William Bernhardt is the bestselling author of *Criminal Intent* and *Final Round*. He has twice won the Oklahoma Book Award for Best Fiction.

Leslie Glass is the beloved author of *Tracking Time*, the newest novel of suspense in her popular April Woo series.

Gini Hartzmark taps into her law and business backgrounds to create the engrossing Kate Millholland legal thrillers. Her most recent novel is *Dead Certain*.

New York Times bestselling author **John Katzenbach** is the author of eight acclaimed novels of suspense, including *Hart's War*, *The Shadow Man*, *Just Cause*, and *The Analyst*.

John Lescroart is a bestselling author of suspense. His novels include *Nothing but the Truth*, *The 13th Juror*, *The Mercy Rule*, and *The Hearing*. His most recent book is *The Oath*.

Bonnie MacDougal is a trial attorney who adds authenticity to everything she writes. She is the author of three novels: *Breach of Promise*, *Angle of Impact*, and *Out of Order*.

Phillip Margolin is the Edgar Award–nominated author of *Wild Justice* and *The Associate*. He was a practicing criminal defense attorney for twenty years.

Brad Meltzer is the *New York Times* bestselling author of *The Tenth Justice*, *Dead Even*, and *The First Counsel*. His newest novel is *The Millionaires*.

Michael Palmer is a master of the medical thriller whose books have been translated into thirty languages. His most recent book is *The Patient*.

New York Times bestselling author **Lisa Scottoline** won the prestigious Edgar Award for *Final Appeal*. Her newest legal thriller is *The Vendetta Defense*.

Laurence Shames is the author of *Mangrove Squeeze*, *Welcome to Paradise*, and other hilarious novels set in Key West. His most recent thriller unveils *The Naked Detective*.

"THIS BOOK DEFINITELY NEEDS TO BE READ AND SAVORED."
—*The Anniston Star*

"It is a smashing story that defies predictability and is a testimony to the talented authors who pull it off. . . . Keeps the readers guessing till the end . . . It's quite a lineup of authors, and the reader wins."
—*Tulsa World*

"Fun and devilish . . . William Bernhardt has hit pay dirt. . . . What they concocted is a seamlessly flowing read that's delightfully over the top, like a *Seinfeld* episode. . . . The trial and ensuing events bring all sorts of harrowing drama and cliffhangers that only a group of clever authors can create. . . . You won't be able to put it down."
—*Arizona Daily Star*

"[A] unique, fun–to–read thriller."
—*Portland Oregonian*

"*Natural Suspect*, with its consistently comic tone, is the best of the 2001 crop."
—*The Weekly Standard*

"A one–of–a–kind thriller . . . A delightful read of a unique nature."
—*Abilene Reporter-News*

"The story has a lot of charm."
—*Booklist*

By William Bernhardt
Published by Ballantine Books:

PRIMARY JUSTICE
BLIND JUSTICE
DEADLY JUSTICE
PERFECT JUSTICE
CRUEL JUSTICE
NAKED JUSTICE
EXTREME JUSTICE
DARK JUSTICE
SILENT JUSTICE
MURDER ONE
CRIMINAL INTENT

DOUBLE JEOPARDY
THE MIDNIGHT BEFORE CHRISTMAS
THE CODE OF BUDDYHOOD
LEGAL BRIEFS
NATURAL SUSPECT
FINAL ROUND

NATURAL SUSPECT

SUSPECT

A Collaborative Novel

William Bernhardt
Leslie Glass
Gini Hartzmark
John Katzenbach
John Lescroart
Bonnie MacDougal
Phillip Margolin
Brad Meltzer
Michael Palmer
Lisa Scottoline
Laurence Shames

Presented by William Bernhardt

BALLANTINE BOOKS • NEW YORK

A Ballantine Book
Published by The Ballantine Publishing Group

Copyright © 2001 by William Bernhardt, Leslie Glass, Gini Hartzmark, John Katzenbach, John Lescroart, Bonnie MacDougal, Phillip Margolin, Brad Meltzer, Michael Palmer, Lisa Scottoline, Laurence Shames

www.ballantinebooks.com

ISBN 0-345-43769-1

Manufactured in the United States of America

First Hardcover Edition: December 2001
First Mass Market Edition: August 2002

OPM   10   9   8   7   6   5   4   3   2   1

CHAPTER

1

SUNDAY AFTERNOON. A time when families all across the country spend quality time together—breaking bread, acknowledging how important they are to one another, sharing secrets. And the Hightower family, one of the richest broods on Long Island, was no exception.

"Who made the martinis?" Marilyn said as she sipped the drink she had just poured out of the tumbler.

"Mummy," Morgan replied, not looking up from his magazine. "Why do you ask?"

"Because as far as I can tell, it's straight gin."

Morgan nodded. "That's our Mummy." Morgan and Marilyn were brother and sister. Morgan was six feet tall, underweight, and carried himself with an air of determined dissipation. Marilyn was almost as tall and was often described as having "steely good looks," which meant both that she was uncommonly attractive and that her beauty was encased in a titanium shell no one had yet managed to penetrate. Morgan was a year older; they were both well into their thirties.

Marilyn poured her drink into the sink, took a tall glass, and reached for a Coke bottle. "That was a bit strong for the first drink of the day."

"Mummy's first drink of the day came shortly after breakfast. What you sampled would be the—oh, I don't know—third or fourth batch of the day. Which might explain why she didn't detect any subtle variations in flavor."

"Toodle-doo, Morgan. Can I come in?" The voice in the hallway came from Cecilia, better known as Sissy, Morgan's well-proportioned wife. She was not generally considered nuclear scientist material, but what she had downstairs compensated Morgan for what she didn't have upstairs, or so everyone assumed, anyway.

Sissy snuggled up beside Morgan, who wrapped his arm around her. "What's my little Morgy doing?"

Morgan had the look of supreme boredom down cold. "Reading, obviously."

She pressed against him. "Could I interest Morgy in doing something a little more . . . athletic?"

"I'm reading, dear."

She brushed her lips against his cheek. "I can think of something more fun than reading."

A pained expression crossed Morgan's face. "Not now, dear. My sinuses are acting up."

"Please?" She traced a line up his neck with her finger, ending at his mouth. "I'll make it worth Morgy-Worgy's time."

"Morgan," Marilyn said sternly. "Be a dear and take your nymphet bride to your bedroom. If I have to listen to any more of this, I'm going to vomit."

"Oh, all right." He laid his magazine down and sighed heavily. "Back to the salt mines."

Before he could move, however, he heard galumphing footsteps signaling that his father was on his way. And that he wasn't in a good mood.

"Has anyone seen Julia?" Morgan and Marilyn's father, Arthur Hightower, was an overweight bear of a man. He was blunt, gruff, and willfully unvarnished. He'd made a fortune in the oil business while the boom was on and managed to keep it when the boom was over. "How long must a man go on searching for his own wife?" He throttled up the volume. "Julia!"

The blanket on the sofa beside Sissy moved. Sissy let out a short, high-pitched cry.

Morgan attempted concern. "What's wrong, dearest?"

"The blanket moved!"

The blanket did move. And then it moved again. And a few moments later, a head peered out over the top. "Did someone call me?"

It was Julia, Morgan and Marilyn's mother. Her hair was mussed, and what they could see of her clothes looked as if she'd been wearing them for days.

"Mummy!" Morgan said. "How long have you been there?"

She took a long time before answering. "What time is it?"

"Almost seven."

Her head bobbed slowly. "Where did the afternoon go?"

Morgan crouched beside the sofa and helped her sit upright. "Are you all right, Mummy? It's nearly time for dinner."

"Forget dinner." Her voice was harsh and raspy. "Where's my martini?"

Morgan rushed to the wet bar to fix it.

"Well, I'm glad I've found you all gathered together in one place," Hightower said. "I've got something on my mind and I want you all to hear it."

"Could it possibly wait, Daddy?" Marilyn asked. "It's time for dinner. And I'm famished."

Hightower made a *hmmph*ing noise. "And I suppose we'll be having the usual twelve-course meal. You children don't know how lucky you are. There were no big face feeds when I was a boy, that's for certain."

Morgan's eyelids drooped. "Here we go . . ."

"When I was growing up on that hardscrabble farm in Omega County in a family of nine, we were poor, and I'm not afraid to admit it. Poor, that's the only word for it. Dirt poor, if you don't mind my saying so. We never had enough to eat. Most nights, I went to bed hungry."

"You've certainly compensated for it in the intervening years," his wife observed.

He didn't hear her, or at any rate, didn't let it check his monologue. "We only had meat once a week. Can you imagine? Only once a week—if we were lucky. For Sunday dinner, my poor mother would fix a chicken. One scrawny little chicken. To be split by the nine of us. You know what piece I always got?"

Marilyn's long lashes fluttered. "Would that perhaps be . . . the feet?"

"That's right," Hightower said. "The feet. I'll bet you didn't even know the feet were edible."

"Only since I was two."

"There's not much meat on the feet, I don't mind

telling you. Not much meat at all. But I didn't complain. No, sir. I was glad to get it."

"I've heard that in Paris," Marilyn said, just to be evil, "chicken feet are all the rage. They're considered quite a delicacy."

Hightower repeated his *hmmph*ing. "Perhaps in Paris, where they'll eat anything if it has enough sauce poured on top of it. But not in Omega County. No, sir. Not a bit of it."

"I've never had chicken's feet," Sissy said, giggling. "But I had frog's legs once. And they tasted like chicken."

Marilyn bit down on her lower lip, struggling to maintain control.

"You children don't appreciate how privileged you are. Never learned the value of money, that's what it is. You're spoiled. Spoiled rotten. I don't know how it happened, but that's what it amounts to. Spoiled."

Marilyn decided the time had come to add some rum to her Coke. "I think that's a bit harsh, Daddykins."

"Maybe it is, but I'm just a poor boy from a hardscrabble farm in Omega County, and I never learned to put on airs or mince words. I call 'em like I see 'em. And when my children are spoiled, I'm not afraid to say so. Not a one of you has ever worked a day in your life."

"Now, Father," Morgan said, "that's not true. I take my work very seriously."

Marilyn snorted into her glass. "Your work? Puh-leese."

The bridge of Morgan's nose crinkled. "Marilyn, you know I've always been very dedicated to my art."

"Art? Goopy watercolors of sunrises are not art."

Morgan's chin rose. "There are certain critics who would differ with you. May I remind you that my art has had a private showing in an important gallery?"

"Yes, a gallery that Daddy owns. When was the last time you completed a painting, anyway? The Carter administration?"

"Every great artist goes through a difficult period."

"More like a difficult decade."

"Enough," Hightower proclaimed. "If this bickering is supposed to impress me, it doesn't."

"Daddy," Marilyn said, "I'm just trying to bring Morgan around to reality."

"You're just trying to be nasty, Marilyn. You were a nasty baby and you haven't improved much in the last thirty years."

"Daddy!"

"It's painful for a man like me to admit it, but the fact is you're all a worthless, heartless pack of wretched refuse, and the thought that I've worked so hard all my life to create a gigantic fortune to be passed on to the likes of you just makes me sick."

"Daddy!"

"Don't think I don't intend to do something about it, either. I'm leaving tonight for an important business trip in Washington, but I'll be back by Thanksgiving, and as soon as I am, I'm having a long talk with my lawyer. I'm not going to let my fortune be squandered on watercolors and trips to Paris for . . . fancy chicken's feet!"

This last bit definitely attracted Marilyn and Morgan's attention. "Daddy!"

"All right, Arthur," Julia chimed in, "that's about enough." The latest martini was sinking in. She was too expert a drinker to slur her words, but the effect was still noticeable in her watery eyes and extravagant gestures. "You've had your fun. I know how you love to play the bogeyman and instill fear in their hearts. Haven't you terrorized them enough?"

"No, damn you, I've hardly begun. And don't think you're going to escape my notice, you drunken waste of time."

"Daddy!" Morgan said. "That's Mummy you're talking about."

"As if I didn't know. Be quiet, you trust-fund troglodyte. Julia, you were a good woman once, but I don't know what's happened to you."

Her voice was deep and throaty. "You happened to me, Arthur, dear."

"Typical. Blame your failings on someone else."

"You haven't exactly been the most attentive husband."

"I've built a successful business out of nothing, if that's what you mean. I've dedicated myself to making a huge pile of money you've been more than happy to squander."

"Oh, yes. Money. Well, that's certainly made us all happy, hasn't it?"

"All I ever asked in return was your affection and fidelity. But did I get it? No, sir. Not even that."

"You haven't got many brownie points in the fidelity department yourself, dear."

Hightower drew himself up like a hot-air balloon. "I never claimed to be flawless. No one who grew up the way I did ever could." He leaned forward, over-pronouncing every word. "But at least I've never carried on with the gardener!"

Marilyn let out a little shriek. "Mother! No!"

"Oh, don't act so self-righteous, Marilyn," Hightower bellowed. "You've slept with every man you've been alone with for more than five minutes since you were fourteen. Not to mention the entire Springdale High class of '91."

"Daddy!"

"But I damn sure never expected to find my wife dancing the hokey-pokey in my own bedroom with the gardener!"

Julia's face flushed bright red, and not from the alcohol, either. "Arthur, please. The children."

"The children. What about the children? For all I know, they've slept with the gardener, too."

Sissy giggled. "Who's the gardener? I didn't know we had a gardener."

"Daddy," Morgan said, "I think you're forgetting yourself. I'm a boy, remember? Er, a man." He chuckled awkwardly. "I couldn't sleep with the gardener."

Hightower arched a bushy eyebrow. "Couldn't you, Morgan?"

Morgan took a deep swallow of his martini.

"Arthur," Julia said, "I think your high blood pressure is getting to you. Why don't you go have a soak in the hot tub? You know that always calms you." She paused. "If you'd like, I could join you . . ."

"Don't disgust me, woman. I'm trying to tell all of you there are going to be some changes made around here. Big changes. Julia, I'm divorcing you."

"Arthur!"

"In fact, I'm divorcing all of you. Cutting you loose. You won't get a cent from me from now on. You'll have to work for a living, for the first time in your miserable existences. It'll do you a world of good."

Julia's martini hand began to shake. "Arthur, you can't mean . . . you don't mean . . . *me*—"

"Indeed I do, woman."

"Arthur, you can't do that."

"But I can, dear. Have you forgotten that little prenup you signed all those years ago?"

The color drained out of her face. "Arthur . . ."

"I'm taking it all back, woman. Every last cent." He reached toward her throat. "Starting with that triple-A imported cultured pearl Mikimoto necklace."

"Arthur—no!" She clutched the necklace, refusing to let go.

"Julia! Give it up!"

"I won't!"

Sissy screamed. Marilyn and Morgan stared at one another, then back at the horrible tableau, unsure of what to do. Hightower continued to struggle with his wife, grunting and straining. Sweat flew off his brow. But Julia would not release the necklace.

"Fine!" he snapped, finally relinquishing his hold. "Keep the damn thing. For now, anyway." He wiped his forehead. "I'll get it soon enough."

Julia fell back against the sofa, breathless. "I need a drink."

"That's right," Hightower bellowed, "get drunk. All of you. Get perfectly potted. Enjoy it while you can. Because first thing after I return, you're going to enter a whole new world. And I rather suspect you're not going to like it very much."

He stormed out of the room, leaving them all in killing silence.

At long last, Marilyn walked to the bar, helped herself to a couple of ice cubes, and rattled the glass. "Well, I'm certainly looking forward to the holidays. How about you?"

*   *   *

THANKSGIVING DAY. A time when families all across the country spend quality time together delighting in one another's company, an occasion for love, laughter, and prayerful thanks. But at the Hightower mansion, the residents were having a difficult time coming up with blessings for which to give thanks.

Morgan, Marilyn, and Sissy sat at the formal dining-room table staring at an array of expensive Wedgwood china—with nothing on it.

"Lovely dinner," Morgan said sharply. "Is there any food?"

"One can only hope," Marilyn answered. "Where's Mother?"

"Three guesses." He made a tippling gesture with his hand.

"Martinis?"

"Except without the vermouth. Or the olive."

Sissy giggled. She placed her hand over her husband's and squeezed affectionately. "I hope she comes soon, lover boy, and brings the food with her. I always work up an appetite when we—" She giggled again, then covered her mouth with her hand. "You know."

"Speaking of appetites," Marilyn said, "I just lost mine. I'm going to look for Mother."

She didn't have to. At that moment, the Hightower matriarch wobbled into the room.

"Has anyone seen my pearl necklace? I haven't been able to find my pearl—" She glanced at the barren tabletop. "What, you ate without me?"

"No, Mummy," Morgan answered. "No one's eaten anything. There's no food."

"Oh." She lowered herself into her seat. "Well, your father always arranges for the Thanksgiving meal."

"Father? I haven't seen him in weeks. Where is he?"

"How should I know?" Julia hiccuped. "Ask Marilyn."

"I certainly don't know," Marilyn said, pressing her hand to her gown. "I haven't seen him since . . . well, I'm sure we all remember."

"*I* remember," Morgan said solemnly.

"Me, too," Sissy echoed. "I still haven't gotten to try chicken's feet."

Morgan rolled his eyes. "While we're on the subject, dear sister of mine, let me tell you something that will chill your heart. I bumped into Joe Kellogg yesterday. That's Father's lawyer. He told me Father had made an appointment to see him right after Thanksgiving."

Marilyn's face fell. "Then he really meant it."

"He did. Either that, or he's giving us one hell of a good scare."

"I've already had a good scare today," Julia said, weaving sideways a bit. "I can't find my pearls."

"You'll be missing a lot more than your pearls if Daddy visits that attorney, Mother." Marilyn whipped her head around to face Morgan. "Do you understand how serious this is?"

"I'm trying, but my concentration is dulled by lack of nutrition. Where's the food?"

Julia waved her hand in the air. "Ask your father."

"Maybe this is how he's going to punish us. Maybe he's going to starve us to death."

"That's the way it always is with you, Morgan. Me, me, me. So selfish."

"Why? Because I want food on Thanksgiving?"

"Even as a toddler, you were never satisfied. Constantly crying. Drove your nannies to distraction."

"Maybe there's some food in the refrigerator?" Sissy offered, trying to be helpful.

Morgan wasn't encouraged. "There isn't. I've already looked."

"We could have a pizza delivered."

"On Thanksgiving?" Morgan slapped his forehead with his hand. "It's Thanksgiving, heart of my heart. No restaurants will be open. Or supermarkets."

"What about that big freezer in the basement?" Marilyn asked. "You got that to store food, didn't you, Mother?"

"I always meant to," Julia said. "I thought if I bought food in large quantities, I wouldn't have to go to the grocery so often."

"Mother, you haven't seen the inside of a grocery store in twenty years."

"Well, the freezer was on sale and I couldn't resist. But I've never put any food in it."

Morgan was becoming wild-eyed. "So you're telling me we have a gigantic food freezer with no food in it?"

"There he goes again. Selfish, selfish, selfish."

Morgan covered his face. "God help me."

"But I think it came with something," his mother continued. "Three frozen pizzas. That's part of what made it such a bargain."

"Good enough." Morgan jumped out of his chair and started toward the basement.

"Morgan!" Marilyn said. "Those pizzas will be something like six years old."

"It's that or cannibalism."

Julia held up her hand. "You'll need the key." She

wobbled into the kitchen, took it off a hook on the wall, and returned.

Morgan snatched the key from her and disappeared. They heard the basement door slam, and after that heard nothing at all. Until they heard Morgan scream.

"Morgy!" Sissy leapt out of her seat and headed downstairs. Her scream was loud enough to be heard in the suburbs.

"Good God, what is it?" Almost grudgingly, Marilyn pushed herself away from the table. Her scream was much more controlled, more like a repressed cry for help. But that was Marilyn's way.

Julia frowned. "I suppose I'm obliged to go look." She wobbled downstairs, using the wall for support whenever possible. The basement steps were particularly treacherous, but she finally managed to make it to the far corner where the other three were still huddled around the open freezer.

Inside the freezer, spread out, faceup, and covered with a thick layer of frost, she saw the frozen remains of her husband of thirty-seven years, Arthur Hightower. His eyes were open, his lips were parted—and he had her triple-A imported cultured pearl necklace clutched in his right fist.

"Great," Julia said. "Leftovers again."

IT MAY HAVE looked as if Devin Gail McGee was sitting calmly at the defendant's table, but in fact her brain was rehearsing her canned opening statement for at least the sixteenth time since breakfast. She'd been working on it all week, but there were still a million unresolved vari-ables. Should she refer to her defendant—that is, her *client*—as Julia, or Mrs. Hightower? Julia seemed more personal, and suggested that Devin liked her and felt intimate toward her, but the honorific reminded the jury that the woman had been married for thirty-seven years and was a member of one of the most prominent families on Long Island. Should she reveal Julia's alibi—such as it was—now, or save it until Julia was on the stand? Should she describe what a miserable human Arthur was and suggest that he deserved to die, or save that until closing? And on and on and on . . .

And none of these questions were trivial. As well she knew, cases were won and lost in opening statements. Juries' first impressions often remained unchanged. She had to make a decision—and she had to choose correctly. Julia had placed her trust in Devin. She couldn't let the poor woman down.

The prosecution's table was still unoccupied, which was a definite cause for concern. Day before yesterday, Kent Conrad, the assistant D.A. who was handling the case, went to the hospital with appendicitis. Rather than delay the trial, the D.A. announced he would assign another lawyer, but as of last night, they still couldn't tell Devin who would serve as lead counsel. This murder was so high-profile that virtually every lawyer in the office had been working on it in some capacity. And there were some Devin would rather be up against than others.

Devin glanced at Julia, who was sitting beside her at the table. She was wearing a simple blue dress with buttons down the middle, as per Devin's instructions. There was no point in denying that Julia was obscenely rich—especially now that her husband was dead. But there was no reason to flaunt it, either.

Julia was a grab bag of nervous mannerisms—a scratch,

a twitch, a flutter with her hands. Devin supposed she had every right to be tense. Who wouldn't be, when they were accused of such a heinous crime, and their very life was at stake?

Devin was distracted by a commotion in the back of the courtroom. The gallery was already packed, so the only likely incoming traffic would be . . . *yes*. Her esteemed opponents. The D.A.'s team was finally putting in an appearance, and standing front and center was— oh, dear God, *no*!

Devin swiveled back around, her hand pressed against her forehead. Was this some sort of cosmic karmic revenge? What could she possibly have done to deserve this? Was it that time she was playing with her mother's makeup and got mascara all over the carpet? Or that time when she was nine and she wouldn't let her cousin Megan bounce on her trampoline? Or did Fate just generally hate her size-six guts?

Trent Ballard was lead counsel for the prosecution, damn it. She hadn't seen him since the trial lawyers' conference at Barkley Beach in May. And actually, she hadn't seen him there, except for Saturday night, late, in the hot tub, when she was wearing that new form-fitting swimsuit she'd gotten from J. Crew and she'd had way too much to drink . . .

"Hiya, Devin. How's tricks?"

Devin stood and simulated something like a smile. "Hello, Trent. Uh—it was Trent, wasn't it?" She almost winced. What a stupid thing . . .

He grinned. "Yeah, no name change since May."

"So you're handling the Hightower case?"

"Lucky me, huh?" The ambitious sparkle in his eye told Devin he really did consider it a lucky break. "I thought for sure McCandliss would keep it for himself, but at the last moment he passed it down to me. I guess he decided it was too politically charged to be desirable, even if the press is likely to be all over it." He took a tiny step closer to her. "But enough shop talk. How have you been? You look great."

Devin deflected the compliment by pretending it was addressed to her clothes. "Oh, you like this suit? It's new."

Trent wasn't that easily avoided. "I wasn't talking about your suit. I was talking about you. You look great. And that business suit can't hold a candle to the hot pink Speedo number you were wearing at Barkley." He flashed a smile that could charm the petals off a daisy. "Although this is probably more appropriate for the courtroom."

Why was he flattering her? It's not as if there were a hot tub in the back of the courtroom. Devin instinctively distrusted people who tried to flatter her. No matter what anyone said, she was never happy with the way she looked. When friends told her she was pretty, she didn't believe it. That's why they're friends, she told herself quietly, every time she heard a compliment. She'd done the best she could this morning with her straight, dark, auburn-tinted hair, but somehow it never came out looking like the women in those magazines. She was wearing her new suit, but new or not, women's business suits weren't really designed to be flattering. No matter what she did, she felt frumpy.

"Look, Trent, if you're going to be handling this trial, it would probably be best if we kept this on a professional basis."

Trent stiffened, and his face took on a mock seriousness. "Of course. I understand completely. We'll keep this clinical." He winked, then returned to his own table.

Devin closed her eyes. Why did it have to be him? Once a man has frolicked with you in the Jacuzzi, there's no chance he's ever going to take you seriously. He'd be patronizing, at best. Maybe even drop sly remarks to the judge, hinting at their dirty secret. Why, why, why?

She flopped down in her chair, feeling exhausted. And the trial hadn't begun yet.

"How're you holding up, Julia?"

Julia tried to smile, but her expression didn't change much. Too many face-lifts, Devin suspected. "Not as well as I'd be doing if that pitcher on the table was filled with martinis."

"Sorry, Julia, but it's strictly water in the courtroom. And please don't try anything sneaky. We don't want the jury to think you're an alcoholic. If they think you were drunk and out of your head . . ."

Julia made a sniffing noise. "As if I would have to be drunk to kill Arthur."

"Mummy!"

Turning, Devin saw that the family had arrived. She had reserved seats for them in the front row of the gallery. She liked the jury to see that the defendant still had the support of her loved ones, although with this family, she considered making an exception.

"How do you feel, Mummy?" Morgan said, grasping her by the shoulders. "We've been so worried about you."

"Stop slobbering, Morgan." Julia shoved him away. "I'm going on trial for murder. How do you think I feel?"

"Mummy, I want you to consider changing lawyers.

Joe Kellogg said he'd be willing to take on your case, even this late. I've asked him to be here this morning, just in case."

Devin looked away and tried to pretend as if she weren't listening. Son of a . . .

"Stop interfering, Morgan," Julia shot back. "If you want to use Joe Kellogg when you're fighting for your life, fine. But I like Devin, and I'm sticking with her. Why do you think I chose her in the first place?"

Actually, Devin had wondered about that herself. No one had been more surprised than she when Julia strolled into her tiny office on Fourteenth Street. There were hundreds of capable lawyers in New York. If she'd had a reason for choosing Devin, she'd never shared it. But given the way Devin's business had been going lately, she wasn't about to turn the lady away.

"Mummy, please reconsider. This is very serious. If you're convicted, they could—could—"

"Stop stuttering, Morgan. They could execute me. Fine. We all have to die sometime. But I spent fifty thousand dollars on specialists to cure you of that stutter, and I don't want to see it all go down the drain."

Marilyn wedged herself against the table. "Is there anything we can do for you, Mother?"

"You could smuggle me in some booze."

"Now, Mother . . ."

"Maybe you could hide it inside a cake, like in those old movies."

"Now, Mother . . ."

She jerked her thumb toward Devin. "The prison warden here says I can only have water in the courtroom. Can you imagine? Water. The very thought makes my stomach do flip-flops."

Devin patted her arm. "You'll get used to it."

"No doubt. And you'll get used to having your client throw up all over the table."

JUDGE HARDY—YES, that was really his name, and no, he wasn't related to Mickey Rooney—was a solidly built man in his early sixties. His hair was gray, but it was all there, close cropped in the prototypical 1950s style. As Devin knew from experience, he conducted a no-nonsense courtroom and rarely so much as cracked a smile.

"This court is called to order," he growled as soon as he emerged from chambers. "Please be seated." He quickly rattled through the preliminary matters. "The first case on the docket today is H01-982, The State versus Julia Conners Hightower. Are all the parties ready to proceed?"

They were. Actually, Devin wasn't, but she was as ready as she was ever likely to be.

"Good." Since the jury had already been selected, the judge was eager to get on with it. He issued a few preliminary cautions to the jurors and the spectators in the packed gallery. Then he called for opening statements.

Devin watched as Trent rose solemnly and approached the jury box. His manner was calm, assured, charismatic. Everything Devin wasn't.

"Arthur Hightower's body had been in the freezer for more than three weeks when it was found. His skin was blue, but you could barely see it, because he was covered by a thick layer of frost. Chipping him out took almost a day. He was so brittle his right arm broke off as they removed him from the freezer. In short, he was not only brutally murdered, but afterward, his body was callously cast aside and mistreated as well. And the woman who committed this heinous offense"—he turned and pointed—"is sitting right over there."

Devin tried to look confident, since she knew most of the jurors would be looking her way. Trent had predictably started with the most lurid—and best-known—aspect of the case. The papers were calling Julia the "Cryogenic Killer."

"Julia Hightower's motives for murdering her husband are well-known and not in dispute. He was planning to cut her out of his will—and to divorce her. After thirty-seven years of living in one of the most wealthy families in the state, she would be utterly penniless. She couldn't handle it. She tried unsuccessfully to talk him out of it. They had a fight, probably fueled by her constant and abusive use of alcohol. One thing led to another—and ended with Julia clubbing her husband on the soft part of his skull with a blunt instrument. Forensic work has been complicated by the corpse's lengthy stay in the freezer, but as you will hear, the coroner believes death was probably instantaneous. After he was dead, Julia dragged the body to the basement and hid it in the freezer. There it remained until it was discovered by her son on Thanksgiving Day—giving him a holiday surprise he likely never would forget."

Trent provided a few more details about the crime and the subsequent investigation, but Devin was impressed by how sparing his remarks were. Some D.A.s droned on forever, as if the race would be won by the attorney who filibustered the longest. But Trent was smarter than that. He knew the importance of capturing and keeping the jurors' attention—and he knew the dangers of boring them.

"One last thing before I sit down. In a moment, you will hear from the attorney who is being paid to represent the killer, Julia Hightower. She will likely have all sorts of excuses and will try to get you to believe any manner of things. All I ask is this—please use your common sense. Don't believe everything you hear. Don't get confused. Keep your mind focused where it should be—on the frozen assets in the basement."

DEVIN WAS NOT pleased. This, she thought, must be what it feels like when a fresh young comic has to go on after, oh, say, Bette Midler. Trent had been fabulous—succinct, dramatic, effective. She wanted to believe the jurors still had open minds, but she knew Trent had effectively closed them, at least a little bit, with his sterling opening. And now she had to stumble up behind him and try to think of some way to yank those minds back open again.

She rummaged through her briefcase looking for her notes, but all she could find was last night's unfinished grid. She'd just have to wing it. She tried to find the friendliest face in the box. Mrs. Miller, perhaps, the divorcée in her mid-fifties who worked at the checkout counter at Piggly Wiggly? Mr. Kimball, the hardware store owner? She settled on Jack Powell, a black man in his thirties who was trying to open his own sandwich shop. He must've seen some trouble in his lifetime. Surely he could sympathize with someone who was in trouble now.

"Let's get one thing straight right off the bat, okay?" Devin looked levelly into the jury box, focusing her attention on Jack Powell. "I'm not here to get anybody off. That's not my job. My job is to provide a defense to the as yet unproven claims of the prosecution. Everyone has a right to a defense, and I'm usually pleased to provide it. But in this instance, it's a particular pleasure to defend Julia Hightower—because she's not guilty. And I'm not saying that because I'm being paid. I'm saying that because it's true."

She took a step sideways and let her eyes drift to the other men and women in the box. Their expressions ranged from politely interested to openly hostile. "Now, a few of the things Mr. Ballard told you are in fact true. Julia does have a problem with alcohol. Of course, when you hear what her life has been like these past many years, you'll wonder that it isn't worse than it is. And it is true that her husband threatened to divorce her a few weeks before he died, although he had made the same threat on many previous occasions and hadn't ever taken Step One toward actually doing it. You see, the late Mr. Hightower liked to threaten. That was his way of keeping everyone in the family under control, and he was very into control. But if this practice was a motive for murder, he would've been dead eleven years ago—because that was when he first made the threat."

She paused, scanning their eyes, trying to gauge whether she was making any impact. "You may have noticed that, although Mr. Ballard proclaimed with certainty that Julia was guilty, he didn't tell you how he was going to prove it. He didn't give you a laundry list of all the evidence he would stack up against her. Why? Because they don't have any. Not much, anyway. They can't link Julia to the murder weapon. In fact, they don't even know what the murder weapon was. Mr. Ballard coyly referred to a 'blunt instrument,' because in fact they don't know what caused Mr. Hightower's head injury. There are no fingerprints linking Julia to the crime. There are no eyewitnesses. All they've got are three mildly incriminating facts—that Julia had the key to the freezer, that some of the victim's blood was found on one of her dresses, and that his frozen hand held her pearl necklace. But those minor details can be explained. They do not prove guilt. And they certainly do not prove guilt beyond a reasonable doubt.

"Because that's the standard, you know. Mr. Ballard didn't mention it; he hopes you'll forget all about it. But I'll never let you forget it, and neither will the judge. In order to convict Julia, you must find her guilty beyond a reasonable doubt. That's a very high bar to vault. If you are not entirely convinced, if you possess a reasonable doubt—then you have no choice. You must acquit. That's the law. More important, that's your duty. Julia Hightower is presumed innocent. And when this trial is completed, that presumption will remain intact. Because she is innocent. Because she did not kill her husband."

Devin turned and walked slowly back to her chair, pleased to hear the heavy silence in the courtroom. She'd made her point. Now she had to sit back and see what Hot Tub Trent had up his sleeve.

"Very well," Judge Hardy said. "We've still got an hour before lunch. Let's get started."

PATRICK ROSWELL HAD learned to read the signs of his editor's irritation many moons ago. It started with the tiny crinkles around his eye sockets. It continued with the subtle flush of color in his cheeks. It flourished with the trembling in his jowls. And it proved itself beyond all doubt when the man began screaming.

"Roswell, what the hell am I looking at?"

Patrick bit down on his lower lip. "It—it—it's an article I wrote up. F-for the paper."

"For the paper? For *my* paper?"

"Y-yes, sir."

The editor, John Whitechapel, stared at the thin manuscript clutched in his hands. He had a squarish head with an extreme buzz cut, flecked with gray on both sides. " 'Fun Freezing Facts.' What in God's name am I supposed to do with this?"

Patrick pushed his thick glasses up the bridge of his nose. "I—I was thinking you might want to run it on the front page. P-perhaps in a boxed sidebar."

"You thought I'd run it on the front page. Of *my* paper?"

"Y-yes, sir."

"What do you think I'm publishing here, *Scientific American*? This is a newspaper. A smallish, local newspaper, true. But we still print news. Hence the name."

"B-but this is news. Or at least—it relates to news."

"What news?"

"The Cryogenic Killer."

"Granted, the Hightower murder is hot stuff. But people don't wanna read about cryogenics. They wanna know who did it! How was it done? Was there a lot of blood? Not what's the perfect temperature for the preservation of human flesh!"

"I wanted to interview the family, but you wouldn't allow it."

"The Hightowers don't advertise in the *Gazette*. Berkowitz Refrigeration does."

"So as long as I was at the cold storage plant—"

"Where I sent you to sell ad copy, Patrick. Did you

forget about that little detail—your job? You're not a re-porter, Patrick. You need to get past these Clark Kent delusions. You sell advertising. And that's important. Cryogenics I can skip, but without advertising I got no newspaper."

"I can do more."

"I don't want you to do more! I want you to sell the blinking ads!" Whitechapel grabbed an open bottle of Maalox on the corner of his desk and drank it down, straight from the bottle. "Look, Patrick, I know you can do more. I run your crossword puzzles, don't I?"

True enough. Patrick had always been fascinated with puzzles, and a couple of years ago, when he turned thirty, he started trying to construct them. Within a year he'd had his first two puzzles published by the *New York Times*. Here at the *Long Island Gazette*, however, there was greater resistance to publishing his creations. White-chapel feared there would be mass reader rebellion if he stopped printing the brainless NEA syndicated puzzle he'd run for years, which was boring, themeless, and wouldn't challenge a well-read five-year-old. Finally, after months of effort, Patrick persuaded Whitechapel to give his own puzzles a try. And as predicted, there were some strong initial objections. Within a month or so, however, all that faded away, and Patrick had a loyal following for his homegrown puzzles. Now if he could only get White-chapel to pay him for them.

"Yes," Patrick said, "you run my crossword puzzles, and they've become very popular. I know people who subscribe to this rag just for my puzzles. Think what might happen if you actually let me write some articles!"

"Patrick, listen to me. You're a nice boy. I've known you

since you were a baby. I knew your mother in high school. I almost asked her to the prom, and I probably should've, except I was all hung up on this cheerleader . . ." Patrick's attention began to wane. He'd heard this story several thousand times too many. ". . . and I want to see you do well. But your highest and best role in the life of this newspaper is selling advertising. You're good at it. I need it. It's a perfect arrangement."

"Just let me take one assignment. One lousy story. You can pick it."

"Patrick—"

"I'll do anything. Garden parties. Dog shows."

"Patrick, have you been out to Hargrove Printing yet?"

"Well, no—"

"Jack Hargrove is one of your biggest accounts, Patrick. You need to take care of him."

"I can still—"

"Have you been out to Mrs. DeBrook's Flowers? Picked up the ad for the Sunday paper?"

"No, but . . ."

Whitechapel straightened. "Patrick, I need you to do your job. If you want to keep your job." He pointed toward the door. "Now go."

THE TINY, SOMEWHAT shriveled man sitting on the next bar stool spoke so softly Patrick had trouble hearing him. From the man's roaming eyes and furtive manner, casual observers might guess he was passing on illegal racing tips, or possibly insider stock-trading data, or at the very least, secrets of state. They would be wrong.

"So," the man whispered, "what about thirteen down?"

"What's the clue?"

" 'Nutcracker suite.' Four letters. Last one's *T*. "

Patrick thought for a moment, then smiled. "Nest."

The little man anxiously scribbled down the word. "What about twelve across? 'McDonald's lid.' Three letters. Starts with *T*."

Patrick barely hesitated. "Tam." He had to hand it to Will Shortz. He came up with some pretty clever clues to spice up the *Times* daily puzzle.

The little man, known to one and all at Murray's Bar & Grill as Henry, continued scratching down words while frequently craning his neck to check the front door. As Patrick knew, it was about time for Henry's new fiancée to drop by Murray's for lunch. Henry liked this woman a great deal, but she was smart and well read and, in his own words, probably out of the reach of a night watchman at Miller Tool and Die. Except that he had managed to convince her he was some kind of mental giant. Which he had accomplished by showing her a fully completed *New York Times* crossword every day. Which he would never have been able to do if Patrick hadn't come to Murray's for lunch every day.

"One last clue," Henry said. "Thirty-two across. Four letters. 'Peter or the Wolfe.' That's Wolfe with an *E* on the end."

"Piece of cake. It's Nero."

Henry finished the puzzle, then slapped the paper down with satisfaction. "Thanks, Patrick. You're a life-saver. What a break for me, havin' a world-famous crossword constructor around."

"I'm not famous. I publish puzzles under a pseudonym—

it's kind of a tradition in the crossword world. Mine's Tristan."

"Tristan? Why'd ya pick that?"

"It's a tribute to my idol: the greatest living puzzle constructor—Isolde."

"Tristan. Isolde. Whatever. I'm just grateful you could help."

"My pleasure. If Cordelia's happy, I'm happy."

"Cordelia's a great gal," Henry said in a dry, raspy voice. "Very classy. Hell of a lot classier than anyone I ever expected to be hitched up with. She makes me laugh." He winked. "And she's a tigress between the sheets."

"Really, Henry, you don't have to tell me everything."

"But she's not interested in gettin' stuck with some dummy. So what could I tell her? I didn't go to college. I don't read much. I don't go to museums and I don't know those ten-dollar words. I thought it was hopeless. Till I remembered my buddy at Murray's who makes puzzles for that big-shot New York City paper."

Patrick smiled. *Buddy* was a bit of a stretch for a guy you only saw at the other end of a bar, but whatever.

"Once I started showin' her those puzzles you helped me finish, she was putty in my hands. You've never seen a girl get so excited about a completed crossword."

No, he certainly hadn't. But he could dream . . .

"Once we're married, I figure I can slack off. But till then . . . lunch at Murray's?"

"Of course. Hey, next week, let's do a British-style cryptic crossword. That'll really blow her away."

His eyes widened. "You think?"

"I know."

The middle-aged woman behind the bar, who Patrick

felt certain was not named Murray, brought his cheese-burger and fries. He was starving. Nothing like a big argument with your boss to work up an appetite. Even if it was an argument they'd had a dozen times before.

At the first bite of the hamburger, Patrick felt as if he'd achieved an altered state. Nirvana, perhaps. Nothing in the world was as good as a good cheeseburger. Nothing. He was gratified that Murray's had such delicious food, especially since he was more or less obligated to eat here every day until Henry finally got Cordelia down the aisle.

The woman behind the counter glanced sideways at him. "Mind if I turn on the tube?"

Patrick shook his head. " 'Course not."

The black screen flickered to blue, then displayed the face of a female news anchor. She was recapping the main stories of the day, using that stilted TV-newscaster voice that always made Patrick cringe.

". . . And today opening arguments were delivered in the high-profile Hightower murder case. The prosecution is expected to put on its first witnesses tomorrow morning. Julia Conners Hightower is on trial for her life, accused of murdering her late husband, multimillionaire oil tycoon Arthur Hightower. Mrs. Hightower allegedly killed her husband with a blunt instrument and stuffed his body into an oversized food freezer, where it was discovered by her son on Thanksgiving Day. Mr. Hightower was thought to have been on a business trip since November second, but it is now believed that he spent the weeks before Thanksgiving"—the anchorwoman paused and looked wryly at the camera—"in cold storage."

Patrick heard Henry make a snorting sound. "Never

ceases to amaze me how much them reporters get wrong. Makes you wonder who you can trust."

"Get wrong? What did they get wrong?"

"That whole business. Rich guy bein' stuffed in the freezer."

"Are you saying he wasn't stuffed in the freezer? 'Cause I've seen pictures back at the paper."

"Naw. I'm sure he got stuffed in the freezer— sometime. But they keep sayin' it was on November second. They say the wife bumped him off and told people he was on a business trip. That's why they accused her of murderin' him. But the man wasn't dead on November second."

Patrick turned slowly. Was it possible this bar rat actually knew something about the murder? "Have you talked to the police?"

"Tried. They told me to go away. Said I wasn't a credible witness. They already had their case worked up against the widow, and they didn't want me messin' things up."

"What did you tell them?"

"What I knew. That Arthur Hightower couldn't've been dead on November second—'cause I saw him alive on the fourth of November. Up at the old Sweeney Hotel. Cordelia and I checked in for the weekend so we could . . . well, I 'spect you can imagine."

"I expect I can. What exactly did you see?"

"Well, it was late, like two in the morning, but we were still awake, and we heard this huge big thumpin' noise from the next room. Shoutin', footsteps, and a lotta other hullabaloo I didn't know what was. So I put on a robe and went out in the hall thinkin' I'd ask the neighbors to keep it down. And who do you think I saw leavin' the room in a great big awful hurry? Arthur Hightower, that's who."

"You're sure it was Hightower?"

"Positive. Absolutely certain. Alive and well, two days after his wife supposedly offed him. And you wanna know somethin' else I'm certain about?" He leaned forward. "He wasn't alone in there."

CHAPTER

2

"Morgy."

"Hmmm?"

"Morgy-Worgy, I was just thinking . . ."

"Oh, don't do that."

Morgan Hightower was in mid-brush-stroke. He didn't take his eyes from the canvas. His wife obviously mistook his muted response as an invitation to continue. "I mean, watching you paint. There's just something so very . . . exciting about somebody dying, don't you think?"

Sissy would have been completely nude except that around her lovely neck she wore a string of Mikimoto pearls that was a perfect match for the necklace that had apparently been the last thing grasped by her grasping late father-in-law. Reclining on a white leather couch with her magnificent breasts exposed in the firelight, she lifted the head of the polar-bear-skin rug from where her husband had placed it between her legs.

"Please don't move!" Morgan snapped in his peevish way.

"But it's so hot there," Sissy replied. "If I just throw off this rug—"

"Even when you have no clothes on, you want to take off your clothes."

Sissy pouted. "There are a lot of men who wouldn't object, you know." The moue gave way to a smile. "Of course, if I get too hot—"

"It's not that." Morgan didn't want to go down that road, not again. "It's the art. You'll ruin the effect."

It was the middle of February, around eight-thirty in the evening. The trial of Julia Hightower had begun that day, and both Morgan and Sissy had been in attendance.

Now, back home, they were in the Rotunda. This was Morgan's artist studio atop the tower that presided over the grounds from the north end of the Hightower Mansion. Arthur, back when he still enjoyed the sensation of being rich and powerful enough to do whatever he damn well wanted to do, had built the structure—a glaring eyesore hard up against the neoclassical lines of the mansion—for the fun of it.

The Rotunda was a large, circular room, entirely enclosed in glass except for an enormous riverstone fireplace that now roared and crackled, giving off an amber light by which Morgan attempted to paint. Outside the wraparound windows, a winter storm had blown down from New England with an arctic chill, high winds, and whiteout conditions. But here in the Rotunda, it was warm and cozy.

Between brush strokes, Morgan was drinking Rémy

Martin XO Cognac from an oversized snifter. He sipped now and looked beyond the canvas to his wife's undeniably attractive body. For an instant, he thought of putting down both his easel and the snifter and replacing the polar bear's head with his own, but then Sissy opened her mouth and ruined it again. "But don't you think, Morgy?" she asked in her maddeningly ambiguous way.

"Think what, dear? Please don't touch your breasts. I'm trying to paint them."

Sighing, Sissy gave a little last pinch to her right nipple, then extended her arm along the back of the couch. "That death is so exciting. I mean, before your father died, you hadn't painted in years and years, and now, ever since—"

As usual, Sissy didn't finish her sentence. Morgan wondered if her thoughts ended that way, too, but then realized the implication of that—that she had thoughts. No, he decided. It couldn't be that. "It's not death, Sissy. It's *Arthur's* death. That's what freed me up. I never understood how much I was afraid of losing the money. Not that money is important to me, of course, not like art is." He sipped his cognac, wondering what was driving him to reveal so much. "But you know I've never had any luck selling my work, or making any money really. If Arthur took it all away, I don't know what we would have done." He took in a deep breath, then let it out slowly. "Now that the worry about that is gone, it is liberating. My creativity can flow freely again. I can actually feel it coursing through my veins."

Sissy had begun, absently, to massage the area around her cute little navel. "And it's good, too, you know, about Julia."

Morgan had started another brush stroke, and this time he did stop midway through it. "What about Mummy?"

"How they won't find her guilty, so it was smart of you to let her . . . oh, Morgy, you know."

"Why won't they find her guilty, Sissy? What did I let her do?"

A look of utter vacancy. "You know, let her get charged and all. When you did it."

"What are you saying?"

"Come on, Morgy. You know!" She threw the polar bear rug to the floor and sat upright. "Yuck! I just hate it when I get all stuck to that leather like that. Maybe we could put a sheet down or something."

"Are you saying you think I killed Arthur?"

Palms upward, she squeezed her breasts together with her elbows. "Well, duh, Morgy. It's not like he didn't deserve it anyway. And you didn't hurt him."

"I didn't kill him, Sissy."

"Oh," she said, obviously unconvinced. "Of course. You have to say that. I know. But I was thinking and I finally figured it out, why you had me go to the Sweeney on the fourth of November. You were trying to protect both me and Julia at the same time."

"No I wasn't. I was planning to meet you there, but my other plans . . ."

"I know. That's what you said, with Joe Kellogg. But I wanted to tell you I knew, so you could tell me if you did. Kill Arthur, I mean."

"I didn't."

A knowing smile. "Okay, Morgy. No big deal. Really. I didn't mean for you to get upset." She let her generous body fall back onto the leather again. "But no rug over me anymore, okay. I really am hot, Morgy. So hot I may need that big old fire extinguisher pretty soon."

"IT'S MY CIVIC duty, Janie. I know it's a little bit of a hardship, but—"

"It ain't no little bit of nothing, Jack." Janie knew that her husband Jack Powell hated it when she talked "black," and this was why she was doing it now. She was angry angry angry, and she wanted him to know it without a doubt. "This ain't likely no *little bit*," she repeated, and then reverted back to her normal diction. She was, after all, making an argument here, and she wasn't going to win by making her husband mad. "Really, Jack. This is a big bit of a problem for us. How are we supposed to get by when you're making eight dollars and forty-five cents *a day* on this jury duty? Who knows for how long? And how's our new shop that we've worked and saved and *slaved* for going to have any kind of fighting chance if you're not here to work it?"

Jack had come to his place of business—Jaksnakshak—directly from the courtroom after the Hightower trial had adjourned for the day, and now he stood in his shirt-sleeves behind the deli case. Thirty-three years old, he was six feet two inches tall and weighed 220 pounds, all of it muscle.

He knew, and when he'd been younger he'd consistently and often proved, that he could beat up just about anybody, and that confidence now resided quietly inside him. He didn't have to talk loud. He didn't have to shove anyone, or clench his fists, or even frown. He knew who he was, who he'd become after a rocky start. He was content with it, and wore that contentment in his face ninety percent of the time.

He really had nothing to prove, except to Janie. He had to prove to her that he loved her. And he wasn't going to do that by fighting. "Work it?" he asked softly. "What does it look like I'm doing now?"

And in fact, he was working. Working hard. He'd already spent an hour on the books and the cash—Jaksnakshak, so far, was only open for the lunch trade, and it had closed for the day at four o'clock.

Now, at eight, the two automatic slicers were cutting tomorrow's paper-thin Italian salami and Virginia ham, and he was peeling the bologna and pastrami for the slicers' next rounds. At the same time, he was wrapping the cheeses—Swiss and provolone and cheddar—in tight packets with Handi-Wrap so that they'd be almost as fresh as fresh cut the next day. The *almost* bothered him, but he'd learned he had to make some compromises.

Janie wiped her hands on the apron that pinched at her expanding waist. The baby was due in three more months, and she was sick with worry. She didn't mean to snap at Jack—God knew he was the best man she'd ever even dreamed of, much less gone out with—but this trial was . . . well, a *trial* for them, too. It seemed such an unnecessary burden, so unfair that the jury summons had come just when it had, leaving so much of the work to her.

Suddenly she realized that the anger was gone. She crossed the space to her husband, put her arms around him. "I know, hon. I know you're working. I didn't mean that. I just don't see why it had to be you. Us."

He held her against him for a minute, marveling at the changing feel of her, the once-flat swimsuit belly now a beautiful orb of potential—their family beginning at last. "Well, Janie, I don't think there's any *why* about it. Me getting summoned just happened." He moved his hands down to her stomach. "You're thinking I've got a duty to this little zygote here, and you're right, but it's not just the store. Long term, best thing I can do for the next generation is be a good citizen, dumb as that sounds. Guys like me, maybe going against type, making the system work, doing what's right. That's the hope."

Janie put her arms around him, so glad Jack was the person he was. She felt the baby move. "Oh, feel." She put Jack's hands on the spot until it happened again. "Okay." Janie beamed up at him. "The bump checks in and agrees with you. So I'll work here and keep this place going, no more complaints. Meanwhile you and this jury make the right decision, hear?"

AT THE OPPOSITE end of the Hightower mansion from the Rotunda, Devin was attempting to conduct a post-mortem on the first day of the trial. When they'd left the courthouse, Julia had suggested that her lawyer drive them both back to the fabulous Hightower estate. Since Devin's alternative was either her one-bedroom apartment in the Village or her drab and depressing (and embarrassingly small) office on Fourteenth Street, she had accepted.

Devin always accepted, she never said no—that was, she told herself, her problem.

Because she believed that no one really liked her, that she wasn't worth liking, she sometimes did things that were not in her own best interest—driving her client out to the Island in a blizzard so she could be in a nice environment for a couple of hours. Sleeping with Trent Ballard.

No! She wasn't going to think about Trent Ballard. Not tonight of all nights.

She and Julia had gotten here at around seven forty-five, and it had immediately become apparent that her client didn't really care for her company after all. And she didn't care about the case either, even if it did threaten her life. Didn't care about her ex-husband, her kids, the gardener.

But she did care about her cocktails, especially after the dry and exhausting day she'd already put in at the trial. Julia Hightower wanted to come home because that's where the gin was.

So five minutes after they'd arrived, they were sitting at the kitchen table—really not much nicer than Devin's own, she noted with some disappointment—and Julia had taken her pitcher from its home in the freezer and filled a glass and started to drink. The frozen stuff poured like maple syrup and disappeared with what Devin thought must be a kind of alchemy.

They made small talk about the case for a while, but Julia's agenda here wasn't communication. Seriously sipping the gin, Devin's client slipped from slurring to snoozing in under an hour. Now, Julia's head was down on the table, and Devin was thirty icy miles from her own sad and lonely apartment, just about ready to cry.

After enduring a few minutes of Julia's graceless snoring, she found herself wondering, and not for the first time, what she had gotten herself into. Also, not for the first time, she wondered why Julia Hightower had chosen her. Out of all the lawyers in the city, why her?

But she could wonder about that as she drove home.

With the snowstorm and the slick roads, she'd have plenty of time. She poked a gentle hand into her client's shoulder. "Julia," she whispered. Then spoke more loudly. "Julia! Let's get you up so you can go to bed. We've got another full trial day tomorrow."

But she might as well have been trying to wake Arthur Hightower. His wife was out for the night.

Sighing, Devin finished her coffee and went over to put the cup in the sink. She opened a couple of drawers until she found the kitchen towels and pulled out a few, draping them over Julia's shoulders so maybe she wouldn't catch a chill. She took the nearly empty gin pitcher and, thinking about it for a beat, replaced it in the freezer. It wasn't hers to throw away. Maybe, she thought, Julia would come to that on her own.

And then maybe Devin would flap her arms and fly to Tahiti.

THE SNOW WAS anything but inviting, and Devin was really in no hurry to be out in it. And here she was, in one of Long Island's grandest houses. It wouldn't hurt to look around a little, she told herself, get a more personal sense of her client and the life she lived, give the blizzard another half hour or so to blow itself out.

The other half lived this way, and she burned to know what it was like. She'd bet nobody here worried about being lovable or pretty. The Hightowers were glamorous. The jet set. Rich and famous. All those clichés. Devin couldn't help but think that though the Hightowers had problems of their own, they were somehow more important than she'd ever be. People who lived in homes like this made a difference; that's all there was to it.

And Devin didn't make any difference, not to anybody. She wanted acceptance here so badly she could taste it. She wanted all these folks to like her. If she could just get their mother off . . .

Well, she reminded herself, it shouldn't be all that hard. After all, what she'd said today in her opening statement wasn't all false. There was almost no physical evidence tying Julia to the crime—certainly the prosecution (Trent Ballard!) couldn't convince the jury beyond a reasonable doubt that there was. Plus, Devin hadn't even mentioned her client's alibi for November second. She wanted to give Trent Ballard a long enough rope to hang himself on the exact time of Arthur Hightower's death— then, if she had to, Devin would trot out the alibi.

By the front door, she stood in a foyer as large as her apartment. High over her head, a huge chandelier glowed with a bright elegance. A majestic staircase curled around behind her, leading to the upper floor. Here on ground level, she pushed the door nearest her and it opened into a dark-paneled library—floor-to-ceiling books with one of those great, old-fashioned sliding ladders to get to the top shelf, a large working desk, a four-foot globe, a fireplace. It was the perfect room, Devin decided. But she dared not stay in it for long.

Across the way, off the opposite side of the foyer, the hardwood floors in the living room made her steps echo deliciously. There seemed to be three or four separate sitting areas, a grand piano, more books in built-in bookshelves . . .

A noise.

She froze, completely still, and listened.

Upstairs.

Male and female voices. Whoever it was, it sounded as if they were having a serious fight. She imagined she could hear punches being thrown, garbled human sounds.

She had to move. If someone were getting hurt, she couldn't let it go on. Out in the foyer, she waited again, heard more commotion, and began climbing the stairs as fast as she could, two at a time.

When she reached the upper landing, she heard a heavy slamming sound coming from one of the rooms off the long hallway. "Hey!" she yelled, poking into the first room. "What's going on?" She was back out in the hallway, going to the next room.

The noises had stopped.

"Stay back!" A woman's voice, ringing with authority. "Stay where you are. Who's out there?"

"It's me. Devin McGee." Her voice seemed to have swallowed her as—too late!—she realized what she had interrupted.

An instant later, the truth was borne out. Marilyn Hightower, disheveled but regally gorgeous in a pale blue silken peignoir appeared. "What the hell are you doing here?" she asked.

"I, uh, I drove your mother . . ."

"I see. And now she's done her passing out routine and you're snooping, aren't you?"

"No, I . . . I heard noises. I thought somebody might be getting hurt."

Marilyn's expression indicated that on the evolutionary scale she considered Devin about equal to, and certainly no higher than, a cockroach. "Well, dear," she said bitingly, "it may be outside the realm of your experience, but sometimes when people make love they also make, well, noise."

Back at the door, a short, gray-haired man appeared in the hallway. Over his black socks, he sported a potbelly and nothing else. He waved sheepishly to Devin, who raised a hand awkwardly, returning the greeting. Marilyn turned, saw the man, looked back at Devin, and smiled icily. "That phenomenal male specimen is Georges Franco, our gardener. Georges, this is Mummy's lawyer, Devin McGee. Now be a dear and go back into the bedroom, would you?"

Marilyn waited until he'd disappeared, then gave her full attention to Devin. "I'm going way out on a limb here and guessing that you're not inclined to join us. No? Well, then, drive carefully and be sure to close the door on your way out."

AND I THOUGHT I was depressed before, Devin mused. Here it is, nine-thirty, I'm stuck in traffic with twenty more miles to drive, they haven't plowed the road yet, I've got to go to the bathroom, and I need to be up by six in the morning to prep for the trial. How could things get any worse?

At that moment, her right front tire hit a brick that had fallen off a truck directly in front of her. The tire blew with a sound like a gunshot and Devin's old trusty Toyota began a slow pirouette that ended in a shallow ditch just off the Long Island Expressway. The car turned a full hundred and eighty degrees around before coming to a stop.

Devin cried. The snow fell and the wind howled and

she waited and waited, watching the miles of headlights creep past her, not one of her famously sympathetic New York neighbors giving even a moment's thought to the disabled wreck on the side of the road.

All of them, she was sure, hated her. And she didn't blame them.

"COME ON, BUCK, come on."

Trent Ballard was trudging in the wind and snow with his boss, District Attorney Aaron McCandliss. Trent had his pet, a twenty-pound giant rabbit named Buck, on a leash, and the two humans waited impatiently for the animal to "do its business."

"Come on, Buck," Trent repeated. "There's a good boy."

McCandliss spoke through gritted, chattering teeth. "I cannot *believe* this. I cannot believe it."

Trent looked over at him. "Normally, he's much better—"

"Damn it, Ballard. Why don't you keep your rabbit in a cage like everybody else?"

"Well, Aaron, in the first place I don't think everybody else has a rabbit." Trent pulled Buck along to a new space a few hops away. "That's why I got Buck. I didn't want to be like everyone else. Besides, it took me months to get him house-trained, and now if I let him go in the house, even in his cage, he'd get confused and revert to bad habits."

"I'm not sure that *confused* is a word that applies to rabbits, Ballard."

"Oh, they're a lot smarter than people give them credit for, sir. Sometimes I think Buck has thoughts, I swear."

"Don't go there, Ballard."

"It's true. And I've taught him some great tricks."

A fresh gust of wind hit them. McCandliss hunched down into his greatcoat. He didn't want to give Ballard any opportunity to describe Buck's fascinating tricks. "I don't care if you've taught him to fly. I care that now we're out in a blizzard in the middle of the night, two grown men, walking a *rabbit*, for God's sake. If anyone from a newspaper sees us . . ."

"It won't happen, sir. Reporters don't like to go out on nights like this."

"Who does? Why are we—oh, never mind."

Trent Ballard shrugged. "Anyway, Buck's almost—ah, there you go. Good boy."

"Is that it? We came out here for that?"

"Well, he is only a rabbit, sir. And usually we do make a couple of stops."

"How about if we don't tonight, okay? How about instead if we go back inside and discuss what seems to be the weakening case against Julia Hightower."

"It's not weakening, sir."

McCandliss shook his head. "Well, it sure as perdition isn't getting any stronger, Ballard. This Devin McGee woman gave a powerful opening statement. And you know we've got some evidence problems she didn't even mention, although she knows about them. I think she's setting a trap, and frankly, I'm worried that you might step into it."

Trent frowned at the criticism, then tugged gently on the specially made leash that he'd attached to Buck's front legs and around his neck. But the rabbit obstinately huddled down into the snow, unmoving.

For an instant, McCandliss considered that Ballard

might have been correct—maybe the rabbit did have some intelligence. Certainly, Buck was now regarding his master with an almost human malevolence—and more intelligence than he ever expected to see in a rodent.

"Okay, you bad boy, no treats for you tonight." Trent gave up pulling on the leash and turned back to Mc-Candliss. "Don't you worry about Devin McGee, sir. That situation is completely under control. Totally."

He gave another smallish tug on the leash, and must have been standing on a patch of ice over snow, because the movement caused him to slip, and suddenly he was on the ground, moaning. Sometime during his fall, he let go of the leash, and Buck—an immovable statue up until then—jumped up and covered twenty feet of snow-covered sidewalk in three leaps.

Through his pain, Trent called out, "Buck! Here, boy. Come on back."

"Ballard!" McCandliss employed his sternest tone. The rabbit could wait, damn it. "Why shouldn't I worry about Devin McGee?"

Trent had pulled himself to his feet and was wiping snow from his coat, all the while using a cajoling voice, his attention focused upon his pet. "Just stay there, Buck. Don't move. Easy, boy." At last he remembered his boss. "Devin McGee? Because I can handle her, sir. Personally." A conspiratorial wink. "A little charm, a little of the old—you know. Piece of cake. I own Devin McGee."

The rabbit hopped again, trailing his leash. "Buck!"

District Attorney Aaron McCandliss watched Trent Ballard—the man he'd chosen for the year's most high-profile murder case—as he attempted to stalk and capture his huge, house-trained rabbit in a snowstorm on a busy Manhattan street. Trent Ballard was confident that he could handle Devin McGee, was he? He owned her?

McCandliss watched Buck jump a few more feet, the superintelligent *bunny rabbit* managing to keep the leash just out of Ballard's grasp.

"Here, Bucky, come on. Be a good boy now. Come to daddy."

The D.A. suddenly wished he'd brought his antacids. His ulcer was acting up. He couldn't bear to watch any longer. But the farce held his attention for another few seconds, and in those seconds, his ace trial attorney Trent Ballard slipped and fell a second time and the old Buckster, the Buckaroo, the Buckwheat Bunny, put another five yards between himself and his master.

"Pathetic," McCandliss muttered under his breath. He turned on his heel and didn't look back.

PATRICK ROSWELL KNEW that he wasn't going to become a famous reporter if he let opportunities like this one get away.

Love-struck, crossword-challenged Henry from Murray's Bar & Grill might be an impeccable source for great cheeseburgers, but as a source for hard news, he was as yet unproved. Still, if Patrick could verify Henry's information about Arthur Hightower Sr.'s condition on November 4—that he'd been alive, and at the Sweeney Hotel—it would break the case wide open. And even more important, it would prove to Mr. Whitechapel that his young advertising salesman had what it took to be an investigative reporter.

But first, he had to endure a long, slow afternoon calling on his accounts—Hargrove Printing, DeBrook's

Flowers, Dodge's Storm Doors, Cornelius Cups and Trophies, Cantor's Custom Accessories, whatever they were. And all the while the wind was picking up and the clouds piled on one another.

He made his last call on Karpfinger's Quality Caskets at seven-fifteen and, since he'd neglected to bring his heavy overcoat to town with him that morning, he decided that he had better go back to his apartment in Little Italy and get on some winter clothes if he didn't want to freeze to death. Somehow, with Hightower Sr. in the news and on his mind, this fate didn't seem as far-fetched as it normally might.

But before he went investigating, he had to get some food inside him. He hadn't eaten since lunch at Murray's, so he stopped in at the pizza place a block from home and ordered a ground beef and cheese calzone. "And, hey, Luigi, you want to throw in some tomatoes and lettuce and onion and maybe a pickle and some ketchup?"

"On a sesame seed bun yet?" Luigi spun his dough in the air, slapped it down on the marble counter, and barked his familiar laugh. "You want, Patrick, I could just make you up a cheeseburger?"

Patrick shook his head. "No, thanks, Luigi. You go to an Italian place, you don't order American. You know what I'm saying? Besides, I had a cheeseburger for lunch. I'm trying to get out of the routine."

"Yeah, sure," Luigi deadpanned. "Well, this ought to do it. You're breakin' new ground here."

Finally, well fed and bundled against the storm, Patrick saw his cab arrive at the entrance to the Sweeney a little after nine o'clock. The hotel, halfway uptown on the West Side, had been recently refurbished, and now seemed to be a relatively friendly place with almost a neighborhood atmosphere. The cab wouldn't turn up the short street to the entrance because it hadn't been plowed, so Patrick walked to where he could see a small bar off the lobby. He stopped for a moment, outside in the swirling snow, taking the measure of the patrons. He knew the reputation of the place and guessed that there were some, maybe many, arrangements beyond those that seemed obvious.

That man in the window holding hands over the tiny table with the much younger woman. The two guys at the bar, locked in a muted conversation, apparently unaware of the television or, indeed, anything else besides each other. The matron and, perhaps, her son.

When it was built back in the twenties, the Sweeney had been a female-only dormitory. Midwestern girls with little or no connections would get to the big city and need an inexpensive and safe place from which to begin their forays into the Big Apple. Naturally, then, the Sweeney had been a mecca for hordes of young men. As times changed and the hotel's fortunes and clientele waxed and waned, it never lost its cachet as a place of secret assignation. Now, in its current incarnation, charming and all spruced up, it attracted clandestine couples from throughout the five boroughs and—if Henry's sighting of Arthur Hightower proved accurate—even millionaires from Long Island.

It was far too cold a night to stand around outside for long. Patrick soon found himself inside, shaking off the snow, hanging his overcoat from a peg by the door. At the bar's entrance, he stopped and let his eyes adjust. The place was smaller and even more crowded than it had looked from the outside. In fact, he didn't see an empty seat.

What he did see, however, was even better.

He took a breath and moved forward between the tiny tables, the undistractable couples, to the end of the bar that had not been visible from outside. One man sat alone under the television set, staring forlornly out over the action. He was in his mid-fifties, handsome, with a full head of graying hair. He listlessly twirled a glass that must have earlier held a Manhattan—a cherry stem on his napkin gave it away.

Patrick didn't want to lose his nerve by thinking about what he was doing. This was a break, fate, call it what you would, and he had to act. "Excuse me," he said to the man as he sidled up to the bar, "but aren't you Joe Kellogg?"

The man slowly turned his head, looked Patrick up and down, lifted his nearly empty glass, and slurped at the dregs. His voice, when it came, was a deep Southern-edged baritone of honey, smoke, and good whiskey. "That's the name, son. But you've got the advantage of me."

"How is that?"

Kellogg chuckled wearily. Perhaps he was a little drunk. "It's an old expression people don't use much anymore. Means you know my name, but I don't know yours."

"Oh, sorry. Of course. Yes, sir. Patrick Roswell, sir."

Kellogg evidently had some code worked out with the bartender, who suddenly was in front of them as though he'd been summoned. Arthur Hightower's lawyer pointed at Patrick. "Manhattan all right? Hit me here again, John, and make it a double. His, too." Kellogg's tone brooked no debate. "Well, Patrick?"

"Manhattan's fine, sir."

"All right. Do I look like I'm in the military?" Eyes on Patrick, waiting for a reply.

"No, sir."

"Then you don't have to call me sir. How old are you, anyway?"

Patrick swallowed. "Thirty-one. I heard that Arthur Hightower was here at this hotel on November the fourth. Do you know anything about that?"

Kellogg looked out the side of his eyes with a spark of interest. "But enough small talk, Patrick. Let's get down to business. You must've heard wrong."

"Why do you say that?"

"Because he was dead."

"That's what they're saying, Mr. Kellogg. But what if it isn't true?"

Hey, presto, their drinks were in front of them. Kellogg picked up his cherry, bit it off, and dropped the stem back into the amber liquid. He moved the ice around with his fingertip, taking his time. "It's true, all right. If it wasn't true, he would have come to my office on the third and signed off on all the papers we'd been preparing for the better part of six months. *Nothing* except him bein' dead would have kept him from doing that. I worked with the man for twenty years, and I know that. You a reporter or something?"

Patrick shrugged, unsure. "Trying to be."

"You wondering why I'm here?"

"The question occurred to me."

"It ain't got to do with Arthur Hightower Senior. And it looks like I'm being stood up." He sipped at his drink again. "You married, Patrick? No, I don't think so. The song had it right. Don't marry a pretty woman. Don't even date one, because you never know."

"I'm not dating anybody," Patrick admitted.

"Maybe I'm not, either. I thought I was, though." His eyes went soft. "Beautiful woman, incredible between the—" He stopped. "But, hell, I don't need to go there." He sighed. "Cordelia."

Patrick felt as though he'd been hit. "What?"

"Cordelia. That's her name. Some handful of pretty woman, let me tell you. And smart? You wouldn't believe."

"Does she like crosswords?" Patrick asked.

"Matter of fact . . . how did you know that?"

"I didn't," Patrick lied. "Just a guess. But about Mr. Hightower . . ."

"No, forget that, there's nothing there," Kellogg said, and suddenly the bartender was signaling again. "Hey, John's tellin' me I'm gettin' a phone call. Maybe it's her. Keep my seat warm, you want to."

Patrick watched him leave the bar and go out into the lobby. After ten minutes or so, he'd finished his drink. John appeared with a second one, saying it was on Mr. Kellogg.

Leaving his glass on the bar, Patrick rose to go to the men's room, and maybe see what was keeping Kellogg. The lawyer was sitting at one of the chairs in the lobby, talking urgently into a telephone. Patrick gave him a little wave and continued on into the bathroom. When he was done, he returned to the bar to wait and nurse his drink.

The bartender had put a little too much bitters in the Manhattan, but Patrick barely noticed. His brain was fully engaged with the coincidence of the name Cordelia, which after all wasn't exactly Brittany or Sue in the common names of the decade department. Could it be that two entirely different women, both of them beautiful, smart, crossword freaks who were great "between the sheets," *and both named Cordelia,* were meeting their lovers in this one small bar? It was possible, he supposed, but not very likely. He'd have to pump Kellogg about it when he got back.

If he ever did.

Patrick checked his watch. He'd finished the second drink and was surprised that it was hitting him so hard. Or maybe he was just tired. It had been a long and exhausting day. He could barely make out the numbers on his wristwatch. He blinked and they seemed to get even fuzzier.

He'd better get up and go see the lawyer in the lobby—interrupt his phone call to Cordelia if he had to—and make an appointment for the next day. He really wasn't feeling very sharp at all. He'd get a good night's sleep and get back on the story tomorrow. That's what he'd do.

But it took nearly all his strength and willpower to negotiate the table in the bar, and when he got to the lobby, Kellogg had disappeared.

Where had he gone? Maybe he was in the bathroom? But Patrick didn't have the strength to go and check.

He couldn't do anything about Kellogg now. He had to get home. Had he had only two drinks? And had they both been doubles? He didn't remember clearly anymore.

Luckily, here was his coat, still hanging on the peg by the door, and then finally he was outside in the swirling storm. Sitting in the warm bar, he'd forgotten how bad it had been outside. With the wind chill, it must be close to zero.

The street hadn't plowed itself and there still weren't any cabs in front of the hotel, but up at the cross street, he saw a steady stream of traffic. It wasn't more than half a block away, and he could flag a hack up there.

If he could make it. Suddenly his legs felt all rubbery. But it wasn't really that far, he told himself. And see? He was already out of the lobby's glow, where the street was dark for a bit. Just a few more steps and he'd be back under a streetlight on the main thoroughfare, where he could flag a cabbie . . .

And then something hit him and all the world went black.

CHAPTER

3

Patrick Roswell woke slowly, the world around him coming into focus like the fancy camera techniques of some graduate-school pretentious art-film wannabe. He was immediately aware that his head was still ringing, but when he tried to lift his hand to massage his temple, he found, to his surprise, that he couldn't move his right arm. This discovery was rapidly followed by the secondary realization that he couldn't move any of his extremities. He looked down and saw that gray duct tape bound him hand and foot, immobilizing him in a hard-backed wooden chair. He also saw that he was stripped naked. A fiercely hot shaft of fear pierced his stomach. He pivoted his head about as best he could to see where he was.

He was in a room that resembled no place he had ever been. The walls were painted a glistening, vibrant white. There was no furniture other than the chair to which he was glued. Out of the corner of his eye, he could just catch a glimpse of his clothes piled in a distant corner. He looked down and saw that the wooden chair in which he was sitting was placed in the center of a large clear plastic sheet. This was disconcerting.

Patrick felt his mouth go dry. He started to cough out a "hello . . ." then stopped. One of the few clear thoughts that managed to penetrate the throbbing in his head and the growing terror within the rest of him was that the only person likely to respond to his call was the person who had brought him to the room, stripped him as he lay unconscious, and strapped him into the wooden chair. He squirmed about and tried to loosen the tape, but felt what little strength he had ebbing swiftly.

Patrick inhaled deeply and tried to collect his thoughts and to impose some order on his fear. I am in trouble, he told himself, which was a statement of such obviousness that it was almost breathtaking. I've got to make a plan. But other than sitting quietly and hoping that over the next decade or so the tape binding him might dissolve, he couldn't see what plan there was to be made.

But I'm not even a real reporter, he silently whined to himself. I mean, if I were at the *Washington Post* or the *New York Times* or maybe even Long Island's *Newsday*, I might be willing to risk life and limb. But I'm not. I'm just a nobody—not even a reporter at a little worthless weekly.

He breathed in again. He fought off the urge to cry out. He closed his eyes, hoping in a childish way that when he opened them again the bare room would evaporate and he would awaken from this unpleasant nightmare in his own ratty little apartment and he could return to his own boring, unpretentious, awful little life.

He squeezed his eyes closed and promised whatever deity might be listening that he would dutifully shelve his every ambition and gratefully return to the mundane world of collecting ads, if only when he lifted his eyelids he was someplace else, preferably far away from anyone connected with the Hightower family.

This, of course, was a prayer that went decidedly unanswered.

He sucked at the hot air of the small room, making a wheezy, asthmatic noise. Patrick slowly opened his eyes and took another survey of the emptiness about him. I am really in trouble, he thought again.

Directly behind him, he heard a door crack open.

Patrick froze, then half closed his eyes and let his head loll forward, feigning unconsciousness, though he thought that whoever was behind him could probably hear the beating of his heart, which threatened to leap directly through his chest. There was a pause; then he heard the door latch shut and footsteps approach. The plastic sheeting made a crinkling sound as the visitor stepped across it.

"Hello, Patrick," said a deep but jocular voice. "Please don't pretend to be asleep. It wastes my time and already you have occupied far more effort and energy than I ever thought I would need to expend on the likes of you. So, please, if you will, let's try to handle the next few minutes efficiently. It would be wise, I think, if you were to consider it important to spend as little time as possible in my presence."

Patrick lifted his head and half turned to see the man with the voice.

"That's better," the man said.

Patrick didn't reply, biting down hard on his lip to keep from shouting out in terror.

What he saw was a large, thin man, probably close to six feet eight or nine, dressed in pale green hospital surgical scrubs, wearing a white laboratory coat, his face covered with white Pan-Cake makeup, a Bozo the Clown bulbous red nose, painted red lips and topped off with a multihued wiry wild wig on his head. In his right hand he carried a briefcase, and in his left a bright blue hard-plastic soft drink cooler. Both hands were encased in latex gloves.

"As you might expect," the clown said briskly, "I have a few questions."

"Who are you?" Patrick blurted out.

The clown broke into a grin, displaying two rows of perfectly capped teeth. "Why, I'm Happy the Clown. Or Jumpin' Jehosophat. Gee Willikers. You can pretty much use your imagination on that score, Patrick. Any appropriate circus-type name would suit me fine."

"But . . ."

"You need to know more?" the clown asked, not unpleasantly. "Well, let's just say that I am the sort of man who accomplishes things. People seek me out because I can straighten out even the most crooked problem. I make things right. Or, at least, right the way they want them to be. I am a fixer and handyman—a jack-of-all-trades for dealing with the stickiest sorts of conflicts. I specialize in the most unusual conundrums and mix-ups that life can possibly deliver. I untie Gordian knots and solve double-crostic puzzles. I am, in short, a good man to have on your side and a bad man to cross. I work outside most norms and conventions, and don't really have much concern or truck with the law. This gives me some advantages in my line of work, Patrick. I am a mechanic for the exotic and out-of-the-ordinary breakdowns on the roads of life. I'm the sort of man who makes obscure riddles clear and thick mysteries obvious. In this regard, I have many, many capacities. Well trained, I am, Patrick, and despite my appearance, not really a very funny man to deal with. Although, I have found that in circumstances such as yours a little levity helps things along. Hence this garb."

The clown gestured toward his nose.

"Honk, honk," he added.

Patrick felt cold circulate within him, as if he'd stepped into a freezing river current. "What do you want with me?"

"Not an unreasonable question," the clown said. He placed his briefcase and plastic cooler on the floor, then knelt down and opened the briefcase. He removed a small, silver dental probe which he flourished in the air between himself and Patrick.

"Is it safe?" the clown demanded in a gruff, Teutonic accent. "Tell me, pliss, is it safe?"

Patrick felt his mouth dry, his heart pound. "Please," he replied, "I don't understand . . ."

The clown frowned. The makeup he wore gave his every expression an exaggerated impact, as if the smiles were in response to something truly hilarious, and the frown a result of some great and utter disappointment. "You're not a film buff?"

"What?"

"A film buff. Don't you like the movies?"

Patrick opened his mouth to reply, but could find no words.

The clown shook his head, making the multicolored

wig bounce around. "I was hoping you'd be a film fan.
Tell me, you don't recognize the late Sir Laurence
Olivier's great line from *Marathon Man*? Where he has a
bit of a discussion with Dustin Hoffman over diamonds
and dental care? Come on, Patrick, everyone remembers
that scene. Unforgettable . . ."

He waved the dental probe in the vague direction of
Patrick's mouth, which, at that moment, seemed to Patrick to be wisely kept shut.

The clown's smile returned. "No? Alas. It does seem to
me that I am running into more and more uneducated
types in my line of work. But I had hopes for you, Patrick. I mean, a newspaper man—or, even an aspiring
newspaper man—ought to be well versed in popular cul-
ture, don't you think?"

The dental probe glistened, reflecting light from a
single, bare overhead bulb as the clown swung it around.
Then, abruptly, the clown stopped the probe in mid-
swing and suddenly pointed it directly at Patrick's mouth.

"You should not be silent when I ask you a question,"
he said, his voice suddenly cold and even, terrifying in its
abrupt flat tones. "When I ask, you should answer. This
will hurry things along and limit your and my involvement. Again, I remind you, this would be a wise phi-
losophy to adopt for the foreseeable future." The clown
leaned forward and tapped the dental probe against
Patrick's lips.

Patrick could feel sweat beginning to gather beneath
his throat, dripping down his chest. The same was true
beneath his armpits. "What do you want from me?"

"Ah, better. What I'd like is the truth. Can you manage
that?"

Patrick nodded.

"I need to hear you," the clown said, a singsong, false menace in each word.

"Yes. Of course. Whatever you want, just let me go."

The clown smiled. "Maybe. Maybe not. That remains to be seen. *Cooperation* is the key word here, Patrick. *Cooperation* and *compliance*. Two key words. Think you can manage those?"

"Yes. Please. What are you going to do to me?"

The clown smiled again. "Why, Patrick, I'm going to hurt you. Isn't that obvious?"

Patrick moaned. "Please, I'll do whatever you want . . ."

"Of course you will," the clown said, matter-of-fact obvious-to-see filling his voice. "I mean, look at you. Look at me. I'd have to say you're not in much of a position to negotiate. You're in a position to—"

He gestured toward the trussed man, as if urging him to complete the sentence, which Patrick did, rapidly.

"—cooperate."

"And?"

"Comply," Patrick added hastily.

The clown looked at his dental probe, abruptly shook his head again, and returned it to the briefcase. But whatever relief Patrick might have momentarily felt at the disappearance of that device was replaced by a new horror when the clown removed a small, surgical steel scalpel from the case. He held it up to the light, admiring it.

"Remarkable, these things. So precise you hardly feel the slice. Hey, doesn't that sound like an advertising agent's nifty slogan." The clown adopted a sonorous mock announcer's voice. "Acme Scalpels. The choice of surgeons all across the globe. Endorsed by ex-KGB,

ex-SAVAK, and former Cali cartel operatives every-
where. So precise, you'll hardly feel the slice . . ." He
glanced at Patrick's face. "Or, at least, that's what I'm
told. Haven't had the experience firsthand, you know."
The clown approached the chair. He placed the blade of
the scalpel against the last joint of Patrick's little finger
on his left hand. When he pulled back, there was a small
cut in the finger, and a thin red line of blood sprang up.

It did hurt, like a paper cut, but Patrick didn't move.

"Brave boy," the clown said, observing Patrick's face.
"That couldn't have been pleasant."

He moved the blade over Patrick's right hand and repeated the slice against the flesh of the thumb.

Patrick thought he might pass out and in that second
couldn't tell whether unconsciousness might or might not
be preferable.

The clown took the blade and moved it to Patrick's
crotch. An involuntary whimper escaped from the bound
man's mouth.

"Yes," the clown said, as Patrick's head spun dizzily.
"That's something to be afraid of, isn't it?"

"Yes," Patrick coughed out. He was surprised he
could make any noise at all, his terror was so complete.

The clown hovered over him, huge, menacing.

"So, now, on to the questions. Tell me what you know,
Patrick. And tell me how you know it. . . ."

"Know about what?" Patrick started, but the clown
merely waved the scalpel in the light so it glistened, then
gestured toward Patrick's groin.

"Please, don't insult my intelligence. You've been
snooping around and digging about, trying to come up
with some information that will help you get a job as a
real newspaper man. You're ever so curious about the

late Mr. Hightower. Now, Patrick, no First Amendment protections in here. Please answer. Immediately."

Patrick nodded and started speaking rapidly. "I know that Arthur Hightower wasn't dead when they think he was because someone saw him at the Sweeney Hotel and I know that he was supposed to sign some papers which he didn't and that his lawyer knows a woman named Cordelia who is dating a guy I know which doesn't add up and . . ." The words poured out of Patrick in a rush. A torrent of discombobulated information, some nugget of which he hoped would please the clown who was leaning toward him, listening carefully.

"And . . . ," Patrick continued, only to stop abruptly, when the clown held up the scalpel.

"Patrick," he said slowly, "you have been busy. More busy than you probably can imagine."

The clown seemed pensive for an instant, as if digesting what Patrick had said. The would-be reporter simply held his breath, waiting for instructions.

"Did you know," the clown said slowly, but then picking up the pace of his words, "that scientists believe that within the next couple of hundred years the human race will no longer be born with the small toes on our feet? They are genetic and evolutionary anachronisms, Patrick. A leftover from our time swinging about in trees. We don't use them for anything except a little bit of balance. So, like all else that Mother Nature finds obsolete, they are slowly but surely being phased out of the body picture. Did you know that?"

"No," Patrick replied, shaking his head.

"Well, now you do. And so, I suspect you won't miss yours. . . ."

With that, the clown suddenly bent down and seized

Patrick's right foot. Before the surprised erstwhile reporter had time even to shout, the clown had taken the scalpel and neatly severed the small toe from the foot. Pain shot through Patrick's leg, black hurt clouded his eyes, he wailed once and almost lost consciousness.

The clown rose, holding the small toe.

"I'll save this for you," he said. He reached over and opened the small blue plastic cooler, which was filled with ice, dropping the toe into the center. "As you can see, Patrick, there is room in the cooler for other digits and appendages."

The clown stared hard into Patrick's eyes. "Don't pass out, Patrick. Your life depends on it."

Patrick was in more pain than he'd ever known in his life. But the agony took a backseat to the fear that washed over him. He nodded.

"They can do wonders with microsurgery, if you want the toe back . . . ," the clown said. "Do you remember John Wayne Bobbitt? Who had his, shall we say, *unit*, severed by his angry wife. They reattached that. This should make you think about the possibilities, Patrick." He held up his hand, stopping any response from Patrick, then reached down into his briefcase. He came up with a plastic bottle of hospital disinfectant, which he opened and squirted onto Patrick's maimed foot. "Now, Patrick," the clown said slowly, "I want you to calmly and carefully describe for me everything you did and heard leading up to your arrival at the Sweeney Hotel. Leave nothing out. Then I want you to pay special attention to accurately reporting what the half-drunk and extremely indiscreet attorney, Mr. Kellogg, so inappropriately told you at the Sweeney Hotel Bar. Think of this as your first real reporting assignment, Patrick. Who, what, where, when, and how. The mantra of the news profession. Safety is in the details, Patrick. Safety and what little chance you have to live through the next few minutes. Do you understand?"

Patrick nodded. He swallowed as much of the pain and fear as he could, and then carefully began to relate everything he'd heard and done that had brought him so close to death at the hands of a clown.

"MORGAN?"

No answer.

"Morgy-Worgy?"

No answer again, except a deep, satisfied snore.

Sissy Hightower rose naked from the bed, leaving her husband asleep. She stepped away, turning back to stare down at Morgan the painter's nude form. He had pasty, white skin, which looked to her as if it could use some time outdoors, and an unpleasantly flaccid paunch. She looked at the arms that had held her a short time earlier, and for a moment wondered if her husband had ever lifted anything heavier than a paintbrush. It was a good thing, she thought, that she had not demanded that he try to carry her over the threshold on their wedding night, because the weakling might have had a stroke. She thought the same might be true if he ever managed to extend the time of their lovemaking beyond thirty seconds.

She walked briskly across the bedroom, pausing only to pick up a red silk robe from a crumpled heap on the floor where her husband had tossed it in a paroxysm of sexual excitement, part of the grand total procedure of two minutes that he'd managed that particular night. She pulled the robe tightly around her near-perfect form, pausing briefly to examine herself in a floor-to-ceiling mirror that did nothing but remind her that she was beautiful in every inch, nook, and cranny.

"Mirror, mirror," she whispered, "on the wall, who's the fairest of them all?"

She smiled, and thought: Don't answer that question. No need to.

At the door to the bedroom, she turned one more time to examine her husband. "At least you're rich," she said out loud. She took note of the empty brandy snifter that had been tossed aside, and the thick oriental carpet of their bedroom preventing it from breaking. Morgan Hightower let out another long, unpleasant snore, and shifted position. "Out like a light," she said. "A couple of drinks, a little bit of the old in-and-out, a shot-in-the-dark, and you're gone for ten, maybe twelve hours." It always astonished her how long the rich could sleep. It was as if having money made them tired. People with ambition, she thought, need less sleep.

She closed the door behind her and walked through the artist's studio, pausing only briefly to examine the portrait of her on which Morgan was working. "Can't even get my tits right," she thought. She shook her head and kept walking. There was a small, spare bedroom down the hallway, which she entered. She walked immediately to the closet and removed a battered old leather suitcase. She took this to the bed and unzipped it. Inside there was a Ruger nine-millimeter semiautomatic pistol, two spare clips of ammunition loaded with wad-cutters, a state-of-the-art IBM laptop computer, some spare clothes, two passports (one American, the other Venezuelan), approximately ten thousand dollars in U.S. currency and similar amounts of British pounds and

Russian rubles, a small jewelry bag that contained an assortment of pearls, diamonds, and other precious stones, a half kilo of cocaine packed in see-through Baggies, and three paperback novels: Thomas Hardy's *The Mayor of Casterbridge*, Dostoevsky's *The Brothers Karamazov*, and John Fowles's *The French Lieutenant's Woman*.

Sissy removed the computer and the Fowles novel.

She took the computer to a small vanity desk, reached underneath, plugged the modem connection into the telephone line, and then sat back as the screen blinked on. It made a whirring noise as it warmed up. Sissy's fingers flew across the keyboard, and in a moment she was connected to the Internet. She typed in her password and discovered an e-mail message waiting for her. She clicked the cursor on the message and read it aloud:

"I have acquired all the news that's not yet fit to print. Need instructions. Discard. Discard with prejudice. I make no recommendation. There are positives and negatives to both solutions. Please advise soonest."

Sissy nodded and thought hard for a moment. She moved the cursor to *reply* and when the e-mail screen came up, typed: *I have no problem with either solution as long as you believe the problem is effectively neutralized. Will rely upon your professional expertise guiding these situations.*

She did not sign the e-mail, but punched the button sending it on its electronic way.

She leaned back in her chair, rocking idly, staring at the screen. Sissy felt she was in an odd state, slightly on the edge of anticipation, seeing things unfolding like a Japanese origami sculpture. She was accustomed to waiting, to being patient, which, she sometimes thought, was her strongest suit. Patience and the ability to stay within character, she reminded herself. She idly wondered why there weren't awards for performers such as herself, who managed to play a role successfully for months on end. The prize she expected was now well within sight.

Sissy sighed. Morgy-Worgy's usual deeply inadequate lovemaking had left her restless, her nerves slightly tingling, as if electric currents were scorching her skin. She punched at the computer keyboard and slid effortlessly into a sadomasochism-and-bondage chat room, where she signed into the electronic conversation as Irma The Bitch. She spent a pleasant half hour taunting and teasing some of the other chat room members, finally making an assignation with some dweeb who promised to lick dog fecal matter off her boots. She told the man to meet her at midnight the following night at a biker's bar in the East Village and insisted the groveling guest wear a pink silk shirt, feather boa, and skintight white pants. She figured if the submissive showed up, the membership of the Village Vipers M.C. would kill him almost instantly.

She signed off the S&M chat room and spent some time linked to a mathematics study group Web site operated by MIT. There were generally some interesting issues being discussed late at night by the next generation of scientists, but this, too, only ate at the hours, instead of filling them. Finally she signed off the computer and packed it back into her suitcase. She picked up the Fowles novel and read for another hour, admiring the complexity of the characters and the situation, as well as the dexterity with which the author slid between past and present. By then it was past midnight.

Sissy stretched, like an old cat aroused from a nap. It

was late enough to go to bed, though she had little desire to climb beneath the sheets next to her rich, untalented, obnoxious, and unattractive husband.

The things a gal is forced to do to get ahead, she said to herself. This made her laugh, inwardly.

She breathed out slowly. Might as well sleep, she thought. Need my energy to get up in the morning and be dumb again.

Sissy replaced the novel next to the computer, zipped up the bag, and secreted it in the closet. Then she padded off down the hallway, each stride taking her away from who she actually was and back into who she was portraying, so that by the time she reached the bedroom she shared with Morgan Hightower, she felt almost as stupid as he so blindly thought she was.

FROM WHERE HE sat in front of his computer screen, Trent Ballard could see that the snow was still swirling down onto the Manhattan streets. It made him shiver and reach over to his desktop to seize the steaming coffee cup he'd placed there. He took a long pull, tasting the bitterness in the drink. It is late, he told himself. It is cold. Wet. Maybe the love-struck and songwriters think the city is beautiful beneath newly fallen snow, but I know that it is merely an immense pain and that for days everything will be slushy, gray, and icy. He glanced over toward Buck, the mega-rabbit, who was merrily munching on a stalk of celery in his cage. "Even bunnies prefer warmth, huh, Buck?"

The rabbit continued to eat, eyeing his master with undisguised contempt.

"Well, soon enough," the prosecutor said. "Soon

enough we'll have some of that nice Caribbean warmth." He grinned at the rabbit. "Buck, did I ever mention to you how much I enjoy a good rabbit stew?"

The beast stared back, still chewing, as if trying to imply that he enjoyed fresh human.

Ballard turned away, fixing his eyes on the computer screen. For the tenth time he read the e-mail letter that glowed in front of him. He warned himself to think carefully before composing a reply. As best as he could tell, everything in the murder case against Julia Hightower was going perfectly, and he didn't want to do anything that might upset that particular applecart. Certainly nothing that might imply that there was something larger going on than simply the highest profile prosecution he'd ever handled. And, he thought, perhaps the largest he would ever handle.

Especially if everything worked out as well as he planned.

Wording his reply carefully, Trent Ballard wrote a few words, then zipped them off into electronic nether-space.

He closed down the computer, reminding himself that the day was fast approaching when he would have to trash this unit and replace it with something new which did not have all sorts of curious and unusual things printed in its electronic hard drive memory.

Behind him, Buck finished the celery stalk. Ballard rose from his desk, oddly energized, feeling no need for sleep. He returned his eyes to the streets below his apartment window. What a mess, he thought. He wondered if anyone official ever anticipated a storm such as this, and whether they planned for it. He thought not. New York liked to react, not anticipate. This was not how he had run his life. And certainly not how he planned to run the rest of it, which, he felt, was starting to look quite nice.

This satisfying reverie was interrupted by the sharp ring of his telephone.

He was momentarily taken aback. It's late, he told himself. And no one is supposed to call me at my home.

Trent reached for the telephone with a sense of disquiet creasing the self-congratulatory image he'd concocted.

"Yes?" he answered abruptly.

The voice on the other end was familiar and surprising. He smiled.

"I didn't think we'd be talking so soon," he said.

CHAPTER

4

GROWING UP IN Queens, Devin didn't get much practice dealing with the dysfunctional rich, but she did learn how to change a tire. Not that the idea of switching out a flat on the side of the Long Island Expressway in the middle of a blinding snowstorm thrilled her. On the other hand, it beat the hell out of waiting forever for the Auto Club to show up or, worse, trudging back to the Hightower estate and asking for help.

She exchanged the high heels she'd worn to court for a pair of thick-soled boots she kept under the seat along with a first-aid kit, a flashlight, and a can of Mace. Pausing to take a tissue from her purse, she proceeded to blow her nose with a distinctly unladylike honk. She couldn't begin to imagine what had come over her. It wasn't like her to feel so sorry for herself that she gave in to tears. She hoped it was a bad case of trial nerves and not an incipient nervous breakdown. Fortunately, insanity wasn't catching. If it was, after her exposure to the Hightowers, she'd end up in the loony bin for sure.

Tonight had been the last straw. Ever since the day Julia Hightower showed up at her office, it seemed to Devin as if she'd been making excuses for one Hightower or another. At first she'd felt so lucky to be given the chance to defend someone like Julia Hightower that she'd practically been grateful to breathe the same air as her wealthy client. During their first meeting she'd had to keep reminding herself to act cool and not stare. It was hard. Just one of Julia's diamonds probably cost more than Devin's father had made driving a city bus his whole life. No doubt about it, the money had done a number on her head.

Pulling up the collar of her coat, Devin opened the door and climbed out of the Toyota into the snow. Maybe it was the cold air, but she suddenly felt more confident and clearheaded than she had in weeks. Lately she'd been thrown by the trappings—the money, the media, the fact that her mother was calling every night all excited to report that she'd seen her on TV. Tonight had helped her finally see what should have been obvious all along. Except for the fact that Julia's checks actually cleared the bank, the Hightowers were no different from any of her other clients.

As a matter of fact, they were probably worse. When you came right down to it, what was she dealing with except a drunk, a slut, and a stupendously bad artist married to a woman with an IQ half her bra size? Even if she didn't manage to get the mother off, at the very least Devin figured she'd be able to get them a slot on *Jerry Springer*.

"Who knows?" she thought to herself as she turned

the key in the lock to open up the trunk. "Maybe he'll do a theme show: Rich women who sleep with their gardeners."

She took the jack and some other tools out of the trunk. If she hadn't seen it with her own eyes she would never have believed it. No way in a million years could she have dreamed up the naked little man and his potbelly. She suppressed a shudder and did her best to drive the offending image from her brain. At least when she'd given in to a moment of weakness it had been with Trent Ballard, who was at least a member of the same species . . .

The ground felt soft beneath the wet snow, still not frozen. She hoped she'd be able to muster the necessary traction to get the Toyota out of the ditch. Standing up, she could see by the light of her flashlight that she had been lucky that the car had come to a stop where it did. A few feet farther and both she and the Toyota would have ended up in a ravine.

Positioning the jack, Devin loosened the lug nuts one by one. The soft earth was less stable than she would have liked, and she made a conscious effort to work quickly. With her dancer's build, people didn't usually think of her as being strong, but when it came to handling tools she understood that skill counted for more than strength. In that way, fixing things was a lot like trying cases.

She got to her feet and brushed the snow from her legs. Then she bent over again and slowly started to work the jack, afraid that if she pumped the handle too fast it would destabilize the car and the jack might slip.

She wondered what Trent Ballard was doing right

now. He was probably lying in his warm bed, dreaming up ways to outmaneuver her in court. Devin had no illusions about Ballard. Hot tub or no hot tub, she knew he would stop at nothing to beat her.

Not that she had any intention of letting him. This case was definitely her ticket, her chance to move up to the majors. There was no way she was going to lose this case, even if she had to get a picture of him walking his grotesque rabbit and figure out a way to show it to the jury. Naturally, she hoped it wouldn't come to that. She knew the state's evidence and had seen the holes in it. Besides, she had a few surprises of her own.

Even though she suffered from bouts of self-doubt, Devin knew her way around the courtroom. She'd learned it by doing Trent Ballard's job, working for Aaron McCandliss prosecuting cases in Nassau County. She also knew that the system was on her side. Even before O.J., it had been getting harder and harder to get juries to put people behind bars.

She blamed it on TV. Starting with *Perry Mason*, television had continually raised the bar of reasonable doubt until virtually every juror in America walked into the courtroom expecting to take part in an hour-long drama. They wanted a smoking gun, surprise witnesses, fingerprints, and loose ends tied up so neatly during closing arguments that the defendant fell to his knees and begged for mercy.

Devin knew what it was like going to court expecting to fight a losing battle with the last six episodes of *Law and Order*. That's why she liked the defense side better. In the end, it was much easier. All she had to do was come up with excuses and change the subject, and the way a good defense attorney did that was by putting someone else on trial. It really didn't matter who—the victim, the police, the stepfather who sexually abused the defendant as a child, or that mythic figure, the other guy, who conceivably could have done it.

Until tonight Devin had been feeling mildly guilty about her plan to use a variation of this oft-used ploy, but after what she'd been through tonight at the hands of the Hightowers, she no longer felt any qualms. Instead, she smiled to herself as she finished unscrewing the lug nuts and dropped them into her pocket so that she'd be able to find them later.

With a grunt of effort, she got down and grabbed either side of the flat and pulled it toward her until it came off. As she dragged it back to the trunk she was pleased to see that the storm seemed to be easing up. She might make it home yet. Working up a sweat, she pulled out the spare and propped it up against the rear bumper while she heaved the flat back into the trunk.

Whether it was the impact of the flat or a gust of wind, Devin couldn't tell, but somehow, something sent the spare tire rolling. Before she could react, it had picked up speed and was heading down the incline toward the ravine. Devin took off after it. She hadn't come this far to spend the rest of her night waiting for a tow truck.

She never heard the explosion. She only felt the impact. It picked her up and knocked her flat in practically the same instant. Instinctively, she rolled away from the blast and in doing so she managed to catch one last glimpse of her faithful Toyota, now completely engulfed in flames, shooting up into the air like a rocket on the Fourth of July.

*   *   *

THE MAN KNOWN only as Stefan wiped the last traces of clown makeup from his face. Even after it was gone it left behind a ghostly pallor that seemed to accentuate the cadaverous hollows of his face. For the few who had seen it and subsequently been permitted to live, it was not an easy face to forget.

A dark scar, crescent-shaped and deep, glistened high on his left cheekbone. As far as the tall man was concerned, it was little consolation that the one responsible had been made to pay with his life. Anonymity was highly prized in his profession and his vertiginous height already presented a formidable challenge. But he managed. The business with the makeup and the wig was just one of many methods he employed.

Still, he disliked the way the makeup caused his face to itch and he was grateful that his next appointment required no disguise. He checked his watch—a Rolex he'd taken off a still-warm corpse—and noted with satisfaction that he was still three minutes ahead of schedule. In his world, staying in front of the curve meant staying alive. In a few days he would have more money than he'd ever dreamed of and he fully intended on living long enough to spend it.

He closed his laptop and slid it into its specially designed leather case. No doubt about it, the Internet had been a tremendous boon to entrepreneurs of every kind, not just booksellers and pornography peddlers. For a hard man used to hard places, it had opened up a whole new way of life, a world of luxury infinitely preferable to the one he'd had in places like Angola and Afghanistan where he'd been sent to learn his trade.

He slung the computer case over his shoulder and gathered up the rest of his equipment—a black leather carpenter's bag, reminiscent of the ones doctors used to carry in the days they still made house calls, and the small plastic cooler. As he bent over, the 9mm that was shoved deep into the waistband of his pants pressed against one hip. He considered it unlikely that he'd be needing it tonight, but complications inevitably arose and it was best to be prepared.

He turned and took one last look around the room. Even though he'd worn surgical gloves, he mentally reviewed each surface he'd touched and subsequently wiped clean. This was, for the tall man, a form of spiritual discipline, like prayer. Satisfied, he made his way toward the door, pausing long enough to pick up the surgical scrubs and bright red theatrical wig he'd bundled neatly into the plastic drop cloth and left inside the door.

He turned the key in the dead bolt and worked it in between the folds of the plastic, slowing his step ever so slightly to deposit the entire bundle down the chute that fed the incinerator in the basement. When he got to the end of the hall he pushed the elevator button and whistled soundlessly between his teeth, his lips spread into something that might conceivably be construed as a smile. He was looking forward to the rest of his evening.

JULIA HIGHTOWER SLOWLY peeled her cheek from the kitchen table and was horrified to discover that she was not merely awake, but sober. It was a condition that she took immediate steps to rectify. Shedding the dish towels that had somehow, inexplicably, come to rest across her shoulders, she strode to the refrigerator with a single-mindedness of purpose and poured herself a drink. She knocked it back so fast that it ended up giving her a brain freeze just like the ones she used to get as a girl back in Texas when she ate her ice cream cone too fast.

"You've come a long way, baby," she said, toasting her reflection in the dark glass of the kitchen window, and poured herself another. There had been a time when Julia had liked to drink, when she'd savored the icy liquor and the way it gradually made her feel all lit up from within. Now when she drank she barely tasted it. All she wanted was oblivion. Unfortunately, there wasn't enough alcohol in the world to blot out the thing that she was most desperate to forget—the fact that she was on trial for a murder she didn't commit.

At least she was pretty sure she hadn't killed Arthur. What with her daily river of gin, things did have a tendency to slip her mind. Even so, she was pretty sure it was something she'd remember, if not the actual killing, then at least the effort it must have taken to maneuver the inert bulk of her dead husband into the freezer. It had been years since she'd lifted anything heavier than a martini glass.

Besides, Julia was the passing-out kind of drunk, not the blacking-out kind—with only one or two notable exceptions. The regrettable episode with the gardener sprang to mind. . . .

Julia drained her glass in an effort to drown the memory. Drinking might not change the past, but if you drank enough, it was possible to achieve a delicious numbness toward the future.

Of course, Julia Hightower had no intention of spending even ten minutes in jail, much less the years and years it would take the State of New York to work up sufficient energy to execute her. She wasn't willing to do it even if it meant saving the necks of her miserable children. Julia had reached an age where she had few illusions and she'd long come to terms with the fact that she'd been a lousy wife and an even worse mother. In fact, the only thing she could think of that she was good at—besides drinking—was keeping secrets. Arthur, more than anyone, had come to appreciate her talent, but if he were still alive even he would profess to be mystified by her silence on the subject of the pearls.

So much had been made of that damned necklace. Julia smiled in spite of herself, imagining the looks on all their faces when she told them that the pearls that had been found clutched in her dearly departed husband's dead hand weren't hers. It just proved that once a woman was past a certain age nobody bothered to look at her anymore. She'd worn her pearls the day before Thanksgiving when she'd driven into the city to have lunch with Joe Kellogg. The pearls in the freezer had to be one of the other strands, one of three identical necklaces Arthur had brought home as gifts in one of his intermittent bouts of generosity. He'd given one to Julia, one to Marilyn, and the third to Morgan, who'd doubtless told Sissy that he'd purchased them for her himself.

Of course, all of Arthur's gifts were tainted. Jewelry from Arthur meant only one thing—he was trying to make amends for another of his sordid affairs. In the simple arithmetic that passed for Arthur's moral code, jewelry—provided it was expensive enough—evened the score. Over the years it had required a lot of evening. The safe behind the bookcase in the library was the exact same size as the one at Tiffany's and very nearly as full. Not that any of it gave her any pleasure. What beauty could there be in a diamond or an emerald if all it represented was yet another in a seemingly endless succession of bimbos?

She didn't want to think about what kind of indiscretion had merited three necklaces. Or maybe it was just that he'd finally found a jeweler willing to give him a quantity discount. By the time he came home with the pearls Julia was genuinely past caring. But that was a hard concept to explain to someone who'd never had the pleasure of being married to a cheat like Arthur. Ironically, it was his infidelities that convinced her that she hadn't killed him. After all, if she'd been capable of murder, she would have been a widow long ago.

She drained her glass and poured herself another. She'd have killed him the first time she found him in bed with the baby-sitter, or that time she'd wandered into the study and found him behind his desk with a beatific smile upon his face. It wasn't until she happened to notice a single stiletto heel protruding from beneath the desk that she discovered the true source of his happiness—a fifteen-year-old hooker he'd picked up on his way home from the city the way another man might have stopped for a six-pack of beer.

Of course, that was nothing compared to the time she'd been playing bridge at the Club and that pretty black girl showed up, heavily pregnant, and explained to Julia and her scandalized friends that she was carrying Arthur's baby. Julia wondered what had become of her—and the child. No doubt Joe Kellogg had made some kind of arrangement.

The thought of Joe Kellogg brought Julia's own attorney to mind. Devin McGee. What sort of name was Devin anyway? What were these mothers thinking? But that was beside the point. The truth is, whenever Julia gave any thought to her attorney (which admittedly was seldom) she felt the teeniest little twinge of guilt. It was too bad so much depended on her being less than frank with Ms. McGee.

Not that she spent much time worrying about the outcome of the trial. She laid her head back down on the kitchen table, feeling the world slipping deliciously away like a gently receding tide. Even if she didn't manage to drink herself to death, for a woman of Julia's means there would always be other avenues of escape. . . .

TRENT BALLARD RACED around the apartment, hurrying to get everything ready. The minute he'd hung up the phone he'd put away his trial notes, tidied up the apartment, put a bottle of champagne on ice, fluffed the pillows on the couch, and brushed his teeth. He was just about to drop a blanket over the top of Buck's cage when he heard the doorbell ring.

"Life is chock-full of surprises," he thought to himself as he stopped in the bathroom to check his hair in the mirror one last time. "Some of them more pleasant than others."

He opened the door and stepped back to let Marilyn Hightower pass. She was dressed for the storm in a floor-length sable coat, and the flakes of snow that clung to the spectacular tumble of her hair glistened in the soft light. Trent's heart hammered in his chest with anticipation. If anything, it seemed to get worse every time.

Marilyn swept into the apartment and cast her eyes imperiously around the room. Ballard felt his throat constrict. It really was amazing, he thought to himself, that a woman who carried herself so regally should have such gutter appetites in bed. No doubt, the contrast was part of the appeal, as was the fact that the woman was practically insatiable. There was nothing she wouldn't do and nobody she wouldn't do it with. Trent would have to pace himself.

Without uttering a word Marilyn Hightower reached for her throat and began slowly to unfasten the buttons of her coat, one after another until finally the priceless fur slid down her body to the floor. Underneath she was dressed only in fishnet stockings that stopped at mid-thigh and high black leather boots with four-inch heels. Her breasts were absolute perfection, round alabaster globes that haunted his every waking hour.

Eagerly he took a step toward the rabbit's cage, anxious to drop the blanket on Buck so that he would be free to give Marilyn and her breasts the attention they deserved.

"Don't," she commanded in a husky whisper. "You know I like it when he watches."

JANIE POWELL WAS so tired she could have lain down on the restaurant floor and happily gone to sleep. It may not have been as comfortable as her bed at home, but she knew for a fact that it was every bit as clean. She'd just finished scrubbing it down herself, proud of the fact that Jaksnakshak was tidy, spotless, and nearly ready for business. All that was left was for Jack to bring up one last case of frozen chicken patties from the big freezer in the basement and they could finally go home.

As much as she hated to admit it, her pregnancy was starting to slow her down. She was doing everything she could to hide her exhaustion from Jack, but she wasn't sure how long she was going to be able to keep it up. Her mother kept telling Janie that she needed to stay off of her feet, that she needed to save her energy for after the baby came, but rest was a luxury that Janie couldn't afford right now. Later, after the damned trial was over . . .

Maybe she would just close her eyes and rest her head on the table for a minute. She was about to shut her eyes when she suddenly sat bolt upright, instantly awake, her incredulous gaze fixed on the street just beyond the plate-glass window.

"Jack!" she called out. "Come here quick!" The alarm in her voice brought her husband from the basement at a run, his face full of concern.

"What is it, honey? Are you okay? Is it the baby?"

She shook her head and pointed.

"Look," she said.

"Look where?"

"There, under the streetlight. Can't you see?"

"Well I'll be damned," exclaimed Jack, taking a step back in surprise.

"It's a naked man," declared Janie incredulously. "A naked *white* man."

"What's he doing outside in the snow?" demanded Jack, reaching up to grab his parka off the hook. "There must be something wrong with his head."

"I don't know about that," countered Janie as she continued staring through the glass at the trail of bloody footprints in the snow. "It looks to me as if the problem is his feet."

THE SIGN ABOVE the loading dock said MCGINTY'S MEATS—WHOLESALE ONLY. The tall man parked his anonymous rental next to a white-paneled van with New Jersey plates. It was the only other vehicle in sight, and judging from the scant dusting of snow that had only just begun accumulating on its windshield, it hadn't been parked here for very long. Stefan hoped for John's sake that he'd managed to get everything ready in time.

He left the laptop in the car. If some hapless thief should be unlucky enough to try to steal it, he'd be in for a nasty surprise. Booby traps were another of the tall man's specialties.

Carrying the cooler and his black leather satchel, Stefan climbed the concrete steps to the loading dock. Before he could even raise his hand to knock, the door swung open. John was still dressed in the vest and bow tie that he'd worn behind the bar at the Sweeney Hotel. From the look on his face it was obvious he couldn't wait to get out of there.

"Who picked this place?" he asked as the tall man stamped his feet on the scarred floor to get some of the snow off. "It gives me the creeps."

"Did you follow all of my instructions?" demanded the other man brusquely. He did not care for using operatives not of his own choosing, but it had been imperative that they have someone on the inside at the Sweeney, and there hadn't been enough time to bring in one of his own men.

"Everything's taken care of."

"Then you can go."

"What about getting rid of the . . ."

"Someone else will be handling disposal," he informed him curtly, his tone clearly indicating that further conversation would be unwelcome.

The bartender shrugged his shoulders and headed for

the door. He'd already done much more than he'd bargained for.

The tall man waited until John had gone before making his way down the long, dim, corridor that led to the cold rooms. He felt fortunate that from time to time in the course of his employment he was afforded an opportunity to indulge himself.

Over the years the tall man had come to see himself as a citizen of the world, apolitical and unattached—a journeyman doing a job. His one great love was for the movies. Never before had there been a medium more perfectly suited for conveying the special qualities of violence. For a man in his profession, who'd by necessity been forced to play out the most thrilling moments of his life before an audience of the soon-to-be-dead, the movie house was a refuge, a place where men like himself were, if not exactly understood, then at least appreciated.

As he pushed open the heavy metal door, he wondered what had ever happened to Bob Hoskins, the cockney actor who'd played the mob boss in *The Long Good Friday*. He'd done that animated movie about the rabbit and then . . . nothing. He navigated between two rows of beef carcasses that hung from meat hooks attached to the conveyor system on the ceiling. The overall effect was chilling. It was really too bad the lawyer wasn't the sort to appreciate all the trouble being taken on his behalf.

Joe Kellogg, bound hand and foot and hung upside down from a meat hook, looked anything but grateful. Gravity had defeated his comb-over, and the long strands of greasy hair that usually concealed his pate now hung pitifully toward the ground. Above the wide band of duct tape that covered his mouth, the lawyer's eyes bulged grotesquely from their sockets.

The tall man briefly considered making a joke about hanging upside down being good for the scalp, but thought better of it. Kellogg wasn't worth the breath. Besides, there were things to get ready.

He set the cooler on the tile floor, which was punctuated with drains. Then he began to unpack his doctor's bag of instruments, laying them out carefully on the worn butcher block in the center of the room. The items formed an eclectic assortment, highly personal and chosen over the years through trial and error. Every object evoked memories. The dental probe he'd used to such great effect in Afghanistan. The soldering iron that inspired such improvisation in Jakarta. Some tasks called for specific implements, but in matters like the one before him, it was often difficult to choose.

He picked each one up carefully, weighing it in his hand and examining it minutely before he laid it back down and selected another. Consumed by terror, Joe Kellogg started making wild, keening noises through the duct tape as his futile struggles against the ropes set him swinging, causing the chains to creak. To Stefan, the sounds held a pleasant harmony.

"Ah," he cried, suddenly inspired as his eyes came to rest on the Black & Decker cordless drill. He picked it up and squeezed the grip that set the drill bit spinning. As he moved toward Kellogg, the tall man was pleased to note that the whine of the drill and the lawyer's increasingly desperate screams blended so perfectly, they sounded almost like music.

*   *   *

JACK WAS PRETTY sure that Janie must think he was crazy to go running out into the snow in order to help some crazy white man. But Jack had been a paramedic before he quit to open the restaurant, which meant that he knew about all the bad things that were out there on the dark streets just waiting to happen. He also knew the cops and figured that it would take a lot more than a call about a naked man to get them out of their warm squad cars on a night like this. If Jack didn't do something about it himself, there was a good chance the poor white fool would end up dying of exposure—or something worse—before the night was out.

"Be careful, honey!" Janie called out after him as he unlocked the front door and headed into the street. He smiled to himself at her concern. The white guy was not only less than half Jack's size, but without any clothes he looked like a plucked chicken. Besides, it wasn't as if there were any place for him to hide a concealed weapon.

"Hey, mister!" he called out, trying to get the guy's attention, not at all that surprised when the man took off. Jack caught up with him before the end of the block without even breaking a sweat. He reached out to grab him by the arm and explain that he was only trying to help, when the poor guy whirled around to face him. His lips were blue and his eyebrows rimed with snow. Jack braced for a fight but instead the naked man covered his head with his hands as if expecting to ward off some sort of blow, then he sank pitifully to his knees in the snow.

PATRICK PRAYED THAT this wasn't some kind of hallucination—the woman's kindly ministrations, the snug shop filled with good smells, and the cup of hot soup he kept trying with shaky hands to get to his lips. After bringing him the soup the woman had gone off again, looking for some clothes for him to put on. In the meantime, they'd bundled him up in big white sheets that he eventually realized must be tablecloths.

The big black man who'd saved him had insisted that he elevate his foot, propping it gingerly on the seat of a chair draped with a clean white towel. Even though it was his own foot, Patrick couldn't bring himself to look. The pain by itself was almost more than he could bear. The black man, however, acted as if he was used to seeing such horrors.

"What happened to your toe?" he asked, making it sound almost as if this were a normal conversation.

Patrick opened his mouth, but quickly discovered he had no words. After all, what was there to say? A man dressed up like Krusty the Clown had cut it off with a scalpel and was holding it for ransom. It might be the truth, but it was too bizarre to be believed. Instead, all Patrick managed was an idiotic shrug.

"My wife and I'll give you a lift to the emergency room, but if we could find the toe there's a good chance that a surgeon could put it back on. . . ."

"I'm not going to the emergency room," declared Patrick, his voice high with panic.

"Don't be a fool, man. They'll give you something for the pain. I know that's got to hurt. Besides, if you don't get started on some antibiotics you'll get blood poisoning for sure."

Patrick felt his eyes widen. The clown hadn't said anything about blood poisoning. What he *had* done was read aloud from a fat surgical textbook. Patrick remembered it practically verbatim:

If wrapped in plastic and placed in a plastic container and packed in ice the severed digit may be successfully replanted up to thirty-six hours following amputation. Of course, the exact critical period of ischemia may vary from case to case . . .

He wasn't exactly sure what ischemia was and under the circumstances he hadn't felt free to ask, but one thing was certain. The man with the red rubber nose and the scalpel meant what he said. If Patrick didn't get him what he wanted within thirty-six hours, not only would he never see his toe again, but he'd be contributing other appendages to the bastard's collection.

AARON McCANDLISS WAS starting the day off in a foul mood. Actually, *starting* wasn't quite accurate, seeing as the Nassau County District Attorney had never made it to bed the night before. This fact was remarkable in and of itself. Over the years he'd managed to oversee the successful prosecution of dozens of notable cases, including the recent trials of the retired schoolteacher known as the Mineola Mangler (three separate counts of first-degree murder) and Rose Mary Bevelaqua, the Long Island housewife accused of cutting off her adulterous husband's penis and feeding it to his pet Doberman (assault with a deadly weapon, battery, and cruelty to animals). But up until now nothing—not a single case—had deprived him of an entire night's sleep. It had taken Trent Ballard to do that.

McCandliss found himself wondering whether Ballard had a drug problem. That would at least explain the rabbit. It might also account for his reckless boasting.

What else would explain the foolishness of bragging to his boss about "owning" Devin McGee?

It had taken the district attorney only a handful of phone calls to have his worst fears realized. Ballard hadn't merely slept with Devin McGee; he'd done it at one of the big trial lawyers' conferences under the noses of half the bar. Even if it didn't raise all kinds of legal and ethical questions, the fact that Ballard had been intimate with Julia Hightower's attorney raised all kinds of disclosure issues that could lead to an eventual mistrial. The last thing the district attorney wanted was to be standing on the courthouse steps explaining that they were going to have to start all over again because Julia Hightower had been denied effective representation by counsel. Any way you looked at it, that night in the sack was going to end up biting the District Attorney's Office in the ass—and in an election year no less.

From the backseat of his county car, McCandliss groaned audibly as his driver made the turn onto West Street and the county courthouse swung into view. If anything, there seemed to be even more reporters out front today than there'd been the day before. No doubt it had something to do with Devin McGee getting her car blown up on the Long Island Expressway. McCandliss wouldn't have put it past her to have planted the bomb herself. He'd already said as much to the chief of police, who'd assured him that he would look into it.

As the car pulled up to the courthouse steps, the district attorney straightened his tie and smoothed the temples of his graying hair with the flats of both palms. Usually he went out of his way to be accommodating to the press, but today he dropped his shoulder and pushed his way through the yelping pack like the running back he'd been in college. He'd been up all night working through his options, and while in his briefcase he had three different motions, all typed, signed, and ready to be submitted to the court, he still couldn't make up his mind which one to use.

The courtroom was packed to the rafters with print journalists and the merely curious. It already felt stuffy and overheated. He noted with irritation that Trent Ballard's seat at the prosecution's table was empty. Indeed, he caught Bonnie Morris, the young lawyer who was Ballard's second chair, casting an anxious look over her shoulder, no doubt hoping that he was Ballard.

On the other side of the aisle, Devin McGee was already in her place, quietly conferring with her client. McCandliss noted with disgust that she was sporting a hard cervical collar, the kind of neck brace usually associated with whiplash injuries. No doubt she planned on playing up whatever minor aches and bruises she may have sustained in the blast.

IF SHE'D KNOWN what the district attorney was thinking, Devin would have been more than happy to tell him that he was wrong. If anything, she felt even worse than she looked. It wasn't just her neck. Every bone in her body hurt, and there was a terrible ringing in her ears that had been caused by the nearness of the explosion. The doctor who'd taken care of her in the emergency room said it might be weeks before it went away.

Of course, McCandliss showing up in the courtroom didn't do anything to make her feel better. She knew that as a rule he went to court only when a big verdict was due to be handed down, and then only in order to take advantage of the publicity. She had no idea what his presence at the Hightower trial meant, but she suspected that it was nothing good.

But she had no time to worry about it. No sooner had McCandliss made it to his seat than the bailiff entered the room and declared in his booming Marine Corps bass that court was now in session. Devin rose painfully to her feet, her heartbeat quickening in anticipation. This was it. Last night she'd made some hard decisions about how she was going to proceed. From here on in there would be no turning back.

ROBERT S. RUTLEDGE stood at the apex of Wall Street in every sense of the word. From his vast corner office high atop the World Financial Center he commanded a breathtaking view of lower Manhattan, while as the managing partner of Hammer, Crain & Rutledge he was lord of much of what he surveyed. One of the world's most powerful privately held trading firms, Hammer Crain, as it was known on the Street, was involved in dozens of different businesses and had far-flung interests all over the globe. But on this particular morning, Robert Rutledge was concerned only with oil—Hightower Oil.

On the desk before him lay the investigator's preliminary report on the Hightower children, complete with highly informative color photographs (taken, by the looks of them, with a very long lens). It made for interesting reading, especially under the circumstances. While Joe Kellogg had assured him that he would deliver the votes when the time came, Rutledge hadn't gotten where he was by leaving things to chance. Assurances or no assurances, he liked to know with whom he was dealing.

The fact that so much depended on the outcome of the trial presented its own set of problems. According to Rutledge's sources inside the courthouse, things were not going as well as might be hoped.

He reached across to the console on his desk and pushed the intercom button.

"Cordelia!" he bellowed into the box. "Cordelia, get yourself in here!"

While by no means a handsome man, he'd discovered that each successive million made him increasingly attractive to the opposite sex. That is, with the notable exception of his personal assistant, Cordelia. Impatiently counting the seconds it took her to respond to his summons, he wondered if perhaps he should try being nicer to her. But he immediately rejected the idea. Hell, the woman was privy to his personal financial statements. That should be aphrodisiac enough.

As soon as Cordelia set foot in his office, he reconsidered. If anyone was worth the extra effort, it was the green-eyed beauty who had worked for the last three months as his assistant. With her long legs and auburn hair, she seemed to embody the perfect combination of sex and class. The fact that she seemed totally indifferent to the effect she had on him made her seem, if anything, even more maddeningly attractive.

"Yes, Mr. Rutledge?" she inquired with the aloof correctness of a well-trained British servant. She was dressed in a cream-colored wool suit over a lavender silk blouse that contrasted dramatically with her green eyes. In her hand she held an oblong box, elaborately gift-wrapped in gold paper and tied with a red ribbon.

"What's that you've got there?" he asked, suddenly adopting the teasing tone he associated with flirtation.

"You never said anything about it being your birthday. If I'd known I would have gotten you something special."

"My birthday is in July," she replied with a demure smile. "This just came by messenger for you. I was about to check my computer files to see whether you had a special occasion coming up when you buzzed."

"In that case, we'd better open it," he declared, taking the box from her hands. Like most millionaires, Rutledge adored presents. He held it up to his ear and gave it a shake. "Doesn't sound breakable," he observed playfully.

Rutledge pulled the ribbon and tore through the paper like an impatient child. Inside was a plain box of heavy brown cardboard. He lifted the flaps, quickly discarding the last sheets of gaily colored tissue that separated him from its contents. Cordelia stepped closer for a better look.

"What the hell is this?" demanded Rutledge, his voice clotted with a mixture of incredulity and rage.

Cordelia did not answer. Instead she staggered toward the door. All the color had drained from her face and the back of one hand was pressed to her lips in a caricature of ladylike revulsion. She fled from the room, leaving Rutledge by himself, staring at the neatly severed human hand.

CHAPTER

5

"Is EVERYTHING OKAY, Ms. McGee?" Judge Hardy
asked.

Struggling to her feet, Devin didn't answer. She knew
the judge hated to be interrupted, but she had no other
choice. Last night's explosion changed everything.

"I asked you a question, Ms. McGee—is everything
okay?"

At this point, the ringing in her ears was almost deaf-
ening. *"I'm fine, Your Honor!"* she shouted at the top of
her lungs. *"I just wanted to make sure I could hear you
okay!"*

Her voice boomed through the room and echoed off
the wood-paneled walls. Behind her, a few members of
the press couldn't help but laugh. Even McCandliss let
out a little snicker.

The judge, however, was less than amused. "I can hear
you just fine, Ms.—"

"*I said I wanted to make sure I could hear you okay!*" she repeated. "*Don't worry, though, it's fine. Let's continue.*"

"Are you sure, Ms. McG—"

"*What?*" Devin shouted.

"I said, are you—"

"*A little bit louder!*"

"Ms. McG—"

"*Perfect!*" she shouted.

Scowling at the now-ready-to-burst members of the press, the judge crossed his arms and leaned back in his seat.

"*Did I say something wrong, your honor?*"

"Why don't we—"

"*What?*"

"*I was trying to make a suggestion, Ms. McGee. Considering your injuries and the seriousness of this proceeding, why don't we recess for the day so you can have a chance to recover from your injuries?*"

Devin nodded at the judge. "*That'd be great! Thank you, your honor!*"

Slamming shut her briefcase, Devin whispered something to Mrs. Hightower and took off for the door.

"Nice trick," McCandliss growled as Devin flew past him in the aisle.

"Sorry," Devin grinned, pointing to her ear. "Can't hear a word."

THE TALL MAN known by some as Stefan scratched the scar on his left cheek and cursed the monkey bars for ever being invented. With a forceful stride and a friendly nod, he strolled right past the security guard in the lobby. "What's cookin'?" he threw in for effect.

"Same old, same old," the guard said with a wave.

Stepping inside the waiting elevator, he pressed the button marked seven. As he waited for the doors to close, he didn't lean back against the railing or rest his shoulder against the wall. He just stood there, unmoving, in the center of the elevator. Without a doubt, he hated the physical filth of the public world, and unlike his predecessor, he wasn't into showy, blood-on-the-walls torture sessions. He knew there was much more order—much more control—in keeping it neat. Put down some plastic; wrap it in a nice little box. Don't touch anything. That's the only way to get away with it.

He stepped out into the fluorescent-lit, blue-carpeted hallway and followed the signs to suite 727. There it was—thick black letters painted on translucent glass: DEVIN A. MCGEE—ATTORNEY AT LAW.

Checking over his shoulder, he made sure the hallway was empty. He opened both hands and dropped two bags to the floor: his black doctor's bag and the plastic cooler. Going for the doctor's bag first, he opened the zipper, rummaged down past the blond wig, and pulled out a small, rectangular case that looked as if it might hold a Montblanc pen. With a quick flip, he opened the case and took out a thin, wire-tipped instrument. Sure, he was good at disguises and booby traps, but that was just the tip of the tall anal-retentive iceberg. A man in his line of work also had to be proficient at first aid, marksmanship, computer hacking, long-range weaponry, short-range weaponry, medium-range weaponry, scuba infiltration, Chinese jacks, and most important, lock picking. A silent flick later, the door swung open and the tall man was inside.

The office itself was sparse and uninspired: a small reception area in the front with a few randomly scattered magazines, and a larger office in the back lined with diplomas and a few personal photos. After checking out the layout for himself, the tall man returned to the reception area and, on a hunch, stepped behind the receptionist's desk. On top of the desk was a phone, a cheap black blotter, and a coffee mug. Raising an eyebrow, he pulled open all the desk drawers. Empty. Every one. Not even a stray pencil. Devin McGee may work in the back, but the reception area was just for show.

Proud of himself, the tall man approached the nearby coffee table and picked up a *People* magazine. It reminded him of the severed hand he sent to Rutledge. Was it too *Godfather*? he wondered, checking the always-easy *People* crossword puzzle. An homage is one thing, but he'd rather die than be derivative.

Flipping back to the front of the magazine, the tall man noticed that the issue was dated a year ago, and that the fraying subscription label was addressed to the Dental Offices of Dr. Milton McGee. She must be taking them from her father. How sad, he thought, as he tossed it back on the table. Must be a bad time to be a lawyer.

"WELL?" TRENT ASKED, rolling toward his partner and propping himself up on an elbow.

"*Well* what?" Marilyn shot back. Lying flat on her back, she let the covers dangle beneath her breasts.

"Well, was it better than the gardener?"

"Don't start with that."

"I'm not starting—I'm just curious."

"You're not curious—you're rubbing it in. You're like an annoying old uncle who always tells the same joke." She lowered her voice and continued, "Was it better? Was it better? Huh, huh, huh, huh?" Shifting back to normal tone, she added, "Get off my case already. We've been through it five hundred times."

"Doesn't make it right."

"I never said it did," Marilyn shot back. "I thought you didn't care if I slept with other people."

"That was just a lie to make you think I was edgy."

"Oh, I knew you were edgy—your bunny convinced me of that."

Trent smiled and turned toward the metal cage. Still wet from the morning's festivities, the rabbit shivered, its dark eyes focused angrily on Marilyn. *I hate you,* it seemed to say. *I hate you, meat.*

Marilyn glanced down at her fur coat on the floor, then grinned back at the enraged rabbit. "You'll never win!"

"Marilyn, can you please stop teasing him?" Trent begged.

"Why? Suddenly you're jealous?"

"Of course I'm not jealous. I just . . . just leave him alone, okay?"

"He star—"

"I don't care if he started it—and stop trying to change the subject. We were talking about you and the gardener."

"Actually, we were talking about me and the rest of the populace. And the way I remember it, you didn't seem to mind when it turned you on."

"That was different."

"Only thing different was the number of people in bed. And no offense to you, pretty boy, but you're not half as much fun alone."

Clenching his teeth, Trent tried to play it cool. He wasn't going to give her the satisfaction. "Let me ask you this," he added. "If it was so bad, why'd you beg for another go-round this morning?"

"You mean besides making you late for court?"

"Late for—? I thought you said it was—" He looked at the alarm clock. 7:50 A.M. He grabbed his watch from the nightstand. 9:50 A.M. "What the hell is wrong with you?" he asked, jumping out of bed. "Why'd you set it back?"

"To be a bitch," she said with a twisted grin.

"Don't play mind games with me, psycho queen. It's not funny anymore."

"Actually, I think it's really funny. Hysterically funny."

Trent continued to hop around, struggling to get dressed. "I'm serious," he said as he pulled on his pants. "I don't like being tricked."

She lifted his tie from the floor and dangled it in front of him. "Silly rabbit," she purred. "Tricks are for kids."

He ripped the tie out of her hands. "I knew you were going to say that! Everyone says it! You can't even help it, can you? It's so old and easy, it just comes right out!"

"So do you, but you don't see me complaining."

Trent stopped where he was. "Have you always been such a vampire?"

She pulled the covers over her breasts and grinned. "When we used to go to Disney World, I'd bring a wheelchair so we could cut all the lines."

"You're sick, y'know that?"

"I hope so," she said. "But that doesn't mean I don't want you to win."

Shoving his feet into his shoes, Trent raced for the door. "We'll discuss the rest of it later. Just feed Buck before you leave."

"Whatever you say, lover boy."

The door slammed shut, and Marilyn stared at the rabbit. Its nose twitched with rage. Refusing to take her eyes off him, she got out of the bed and reached for the phone. Eleven digits later, a voice said hello. "It's me," Marilyn explained as she approached the cage. "Yeah. Yeah, he just left. He didn't even think about it—it's just like I told you—typical male." Leaning down toward Buck, she slowly brushed her fingernails against the bars of the cage. "Hold out the right carrot, and they'll always come running."

FOLLOWING THE TWISTING and turning hallway, Devin McGee had her chest out and her head high. Sure, it wasn't right to trick the judge, but . . . well . . . at least it bought her some time. Like her Crim Law professor used to say, "When it's out of your control, get it out of the courtroom."

At the end of the hall, she quickly approached suite 727. Seeing the familiar DEVIN A. MCGEE—ATTORNEY AT LAW sign, she reached into her purse and pulled out a small wad of keys. She slid them in the door and was relaxed by the thunk of the opening locks. The sounds of home. Twisting the doorknob, she thought she heard something move, but as she flipped on the light switch, all she saw was the familiar MY LAWYER'S BIGGER THAN YOUR LAWYER coffee mug sitting on the always-empty receptionist's desk. There was another sharp noise behind her and the door slammed shut—but before Devin could react, a thick, meaty hand clamped over her mouth. Her eyes were still focused on the happy bright red letters of the coffee mug. That was the last thing she saw.

AFTER A TRIP to his apartment for a quick replenishment of clothes, Patrick didn't waste time getting back to his office. Despite his limp, he stormed through the humming newsroom, marched past the unending rows of cubicles and, without stopping, threw open the door to Whitechapel's office, sending it crashing into the wall. Whitechapel was in the middle of his midmorning ritual: With an open can of anchovies in his hand, he was hunched over his desk, flipping through a six-inch stack of various-sized newspapers. The competition'll kill you in New York.

Hoping to keep the conversation private, Patrick closed the door behind himself, leaving just the two of them alone in the office. Whitechapel was so caught up in his reading material, he still hadn't looked up.

"Boss, I need to—"

"Let me ask you a question," Whitechapel said as he used his fingers to pick a runny anchovy out of the metal can. He put it in between his lips and sucked it in with a slurp. "Do you believe in acquired tastes, or do you think they're just self-delusional lies?"

"Actually, I was wondering—"

"Save your wondering—this is an important question." Flipping through the paper and throwing back another anchovy, he added, "For as long as I can remember, people have said caviar's one of the great delicacies of the world. Then last night, I go to this cocktail party and this fella—he's full of a good six or seven brandies—he tells me that caviar is a practical joke that the rich play on the rest of us up-and-comers. Says it's like the emperor's new clothes—the rich say they love it—they even order it for their parties—but when it's passed around, they never touch it; they just wait to see who does. Then when the compliments start flying about how delicious it is, they sit back and laugh themselves sick. It's supposed to be some grand old tradition that separates the haves from the have-a-lots."

"Sir, I don't think that's—"

"Think about it, boy. It's just like Shakespeare said: ' 'twas caviary to the general'—general public is who he's talking about. Me and you. I mean, it's a rotten-smelling mush of fish spew, and we pay two hundred bucks a pound to brag about it on a cracker."

"But—"

"And why should it stop at caviar? It could be all acquired tastes—scotch, modern art, Renaissance Weekend—for all we know, every one of them's a big, fat self-decepti—"

"So what if it is!?" Patrick shouted. "What're you gonna do? Print a tell-all story and have everyone call you a crackpot? Sure, it tastes like crap; sure, we all hate it; sure, we all swallow it with a smile. That's who were are—we want to fit in—and nothing you write is gonna change that. Period. End. Finis!"

Closing the newspaper in front of him, Whitechapel finally looked up. "I take it this isn't about a problem with the crossword?"

"What do you think?" Patrick asked, limping forward. His eyes were hollow, with deep bags below them.

"You were fishing around the Hightowers, weren't you?"

"Boss, before you—"

"Didn't I tell you not to do that? Weren't those my exact orders? I swear, Patrick, from here on in—if they sue us for—"

"Julia Hightower didn't kill her husband!"

Right there, Whitechapel stopped. He knew what it took to sell papers. "Say again?"

"I'm telling you, she didn't kill him."

"And I suppose you have proof of this?"

"Nothing concrete, but I have a source."

"A source?" he asked, shooting out of his seat. Patrick had seen this before. Whitechapel leaned forward so his knuckles rested on his desk. "Who is it? Fatty? Mickey? Rubin?"

"No one you know, but I think he's solid." Patrick took a deep breath. He didn't like lying to his boss, but the clown had been specific. The first thing he had to do was plant a story. Nothing special—just something to raise a few eyebrows. Shine the spotlight. After that, the rest would start falling into place.

"So he gave you solid info on Julia's alibi?"

"Not exactly—but he did point out that she doesn't necessarily have everything to gain."

"I don't understand."

"Don't you remember the Doniger case a few years back—rich Upper East Side old guy drops dead from what looks like a diabetic stroke. Then it comes out that his way-too-young wife and his best friend actually did him in and stuffed him in his wine cellar until they established their alibis."

"I remember it," Whitechapel insisted. "So what's the point?"

"The point is, when it came out that the wife was involved with the murder, she didn't get a single nickel of inheritance. According to New York law, we've got the equivalent of a slayer statute, which means killers can't benefit from their crimes."

"And that makes you convinced Julia didn't kill her husband?"

"No," Patrick said. "It makes me convinced that if Julia Hightower is found guilty, there're plenty of other people who can get their greedy mitts on the Hightower pot of gold."

Whitechapel nodded to himself. "I see what you're saying—if Julia gets convicted of the murder . . ."

". . . then the money goes to whoever's next in line in the will . . ."

". . . which means Marilyn and Morgan have millions of great reasons to kill Daddy and pin it on Mommy." Shaking his head, Whitechapel added, "And people say families don't talk anymore."

"So what do you think?" Patrick asked.

"It's a little out there, but it's certainly possible."

Patrick grinned. "So I have a story?"

"Are you nuts? You have some nice conjecture, but there's not a single fact in there—not to mention the fact that in the Doniger case, the wife *did* kill her husband."

"But the—"

"Patrick, writing a story isn't the same as writing nine-down and eight-across—this is news, my friend. So unless your source gave you some actual facts, all you've—"

"What if I gave you a body?"

"Excuse me?"

"A body. A dead body," Patrick explained. "Arthur Hightower's lawyer, to be exact. My source gave me the location and said Julia had a foolproof alibi."

Whitechapel crossed his arms over his broad chest. "You yanking my ya-ya?"

Patrick looked him straight in the eyes. "What do you think?"

Staring back, Whitechapel knew the answer. He pulled a pad from his top drawer and slid it across his desk. "Give me the address and get your ass over there. I'll give you a fifteen-minute head start before I call it in—that should be more than enough time to make sure you're first man on the scene."

"Great," Patrick beamed, a wide smile lifting his cheeks. "That's great." He scribbled the address, then darted for the door.

"By the way," Whitechapel interrupted. "This wouldn't have anything to do with that limp you got going, would it?"

Patrick froze. "What're you—"

"I'm not a moron, son. You look ten years older than when you left here yesterday, and suddenly you've got better information than my top city guy." Pausing for a moment, he added, "Now, do you want to tell me what's going on?"

Patrick stared at the carpet.

"This source of yours isn't on the up-and-up, is he?"

Again, Patrick didn't answer.

"Is he threatening you—"

"No. Not at all," Patrick shot back. If Whitechapel thought they were being manipulated, he'd bury the story. Besides, regardless of the clown's motives, a dead body is still news. "I promise you, boss—when I can explain, I will. For now, I'm just asking you to trust me. Please."

Biting the inside of his cheek, Whitechapel stayed silent, his eyes narrowing ever so slightly. Patrick could feel the weight of judgment wash over him. Finally, Whitechapel said, "I'll give you the byline, but I want all copy running through me."

"You got it," Patrick said. "Everything through you."

"One last thing," Whitechapel called out. "Why're you doing this?"

"Why do you think?" Patrick asked without looking back. "I want to be a reporter." Before his boss could say a word, Patrick opened the door and left the office.

Limping back through the newsroom, Patrick thought about the real answer to Whitechapel's question. Why am I doing this? he asked himself for the tenth time this morning. For the most obvious reason of all. He tightened his fists and did his best to bury the pain. "*I want my toe!*"

"I WANT MY hand!" Rutledge shouted, banging his antique walnut desk.

"I'm sure you do," the man in the cheap wool sport jacket stated. "But let me remind you of two things: one, it's not your hand; two, and more important, it's officially being cataloged as evidence." After sliding the severed hand and its gift-wrapped box into a clear, plastic evidence bag, Detective Guttman sealed it up like a salami sandwich in a Ziploc and tossed it in a cooler packed with dry ice. On the outside of the cooler were the words LIL' PHREEZE and a small cartoon Eskimo.

Watching the detective in front of his desk, Rutledge clenched his teeth and sat back in his chair. If it were up to him, he'd never have called the police, but Cordelia, as usual, overreacted. How was he supposed to know that when she ran from the office, her first reaction would be to dial 911? Sure, it's a severed hand, but hasn't she ever seen any mob movies? They do this stuff all the time.

"Now is there anything else you wanted to add?" Detective Guttman asked as he pulled a ratty notepad from his jacket pocket.

"I think you have everything," Rutledge replied, his voice its usual mix of strong suggestions and soft threats. "You know it all."

"Thanks. We'll be in touch as soon as we get an ID."

Rutledge nodded and the detective headed for the door. Watching him leave, Rutledge knew he wasn't going to have to wait for the ID. The moment he saw the severed hand, with its JFK gold initial ring, he knew Joseph Francis Kellogg was in trouble. The ring was a knockoff of the one Kennedy used to wear before he was president, but Kellogg used to brag that it was the original. Typical lawyer, Rutledge had thought when he first heard it—always trying to impress.

Buzzing his intercom, Rutledge waited for Cordelia to answer.

"Mr. Rutledge?" she stuttered. "Is everything okay?"

"Actually, that's what I was going to ask you." Before he could finish, he heard the line go silent. Seconds later, there was a soft knock on his door. Cordelia. "Come in, come in," he said, anxious to be near her once again.

She slowly leaned into his office and her green eyes lit up the room. "Sorry to interrupt. I just—"

"Not at all," he said as tenderly as possible. "I mean,

considering the morning's events . . . well, let me put it this way . . . if you need some personal time, you're more than welcome to take the rest of the day off." Smiling to himself, Rutledge knew she'd never take him up on the offer, but as long as he put it out there, he'd be able to—

"Actually, that was just what I was going to ask you," she interrupted. "If it's okay, I figured we'd call it a half day." Before he could argue, Cordelia was back at the door—this time on her way out. The door slammed shut, and once again, he was all alone. He hated being alone.

The ensuing silence smacked him square in the chest—and as the consequences started to sink in, a single bead of sweat ran down the center of his forehead. Whoever did this—they knew what he was up to. In the town of a billion secrets, his most closely guarded one had somehow gotten out. That's why they sent the hand. And while, sure, having it delivered was a bit too *Godfather*, only a fool couldn't see the writing on the designer-painted walls: Like it or not, the rules had changed.

Wiping the sweat from his brow, he reached for the phone and dialed Kellogg's number. It was a long shot, but he didn't know what else to do. He wrapped the telephone cord around his finger and waited for someone to pick up. "C'mon . . . ," he demanded, as if that would somehow affect the outcome. Maybe it wasn't as bad as he thought. Maybe there was still a chance. Over and over, the phone continued to ring. But no one ever answered.

BLINKING HER WAY back to consciousness, Devin could barely keep her head up. Her clothes were on and the smell of old books was familiar, but in front of her, the whole world was blurry—a kaleidoscope of unintelligible shapes and colors. Still struggling to make sense of it, she tried to rub her eyes. That's when she realized her wrists were handcuffed to the armrests of the leather chair in her office.

"What the hell is going on!?" she tried to shout as she struggled against her restraints, but the words came out of her mouth more like a whisper.

"Don't panic," a calm voice answered, causing her to jump.

In front of her, the world slowly, finally came into focus. And the first thing she saw was a tall man towering over her even though he was on the other side of the desk. He wore a long blond wig, a black-and-white vertical-striped shirt, and bright white pants. "Ready to join the waking world?" he asked with a grin.

"Who are you?"

His voice was a flatline—never angry, just calm and cold. "Who am I?" he asked. "Does it really matter?"

Watching him carefully, Devin could feel her stomach spinning and her hands shaking. The tall man let out a thin grin. "Don't fret," he teased. "It's only temporary."

Still staring at her captor, Devin was about to blurt something, but she stopped herself.

"Oh, Ms. McGee, you don't have to hold back—you're among . . . friends. Ask me anything you want."

The shaking in Devin's hands was getting worse, but she remembered an article she'd recently read about hostage negotiations. Always keep them talking. It's the only way to prevent the worst. "W-why're you here?" she stuttered.

"Believe it or not, I'm just trying to create a level playing field."

"Is that why you're dressed like a referee?" It was her way of keeping things light, but as soon as she asked the question, she could feel the mood shift.

A quiet darkness took the man's face and his jaw shifted off-center. "Do you see a whistle around my neck? Do you see a cordless mike? *I'm not a referee!* " he shouted, slapping his hands against the desk. "I'm a female Foot Locker employee!"

She wanted to say something—anything to calm him down—but he was clearly raging.

"Don't play stupid, Ms. McGee," he continued. "All you have to do is pay attention to the details." He reached into his back pocket and pulled out a bright silver shoehorn. "Do referees carry shoehorns? *Do they?* Have you ever seen one with a shoehorn? I don't think so!"

"What're you—"

Ignoring her and looking away as if he were listening to an omniscient voice, the tall man ran his hand down the back of his blond hair. In his heart, he knew it was a good costume, but he couldn't help second-guessing himself. Maybe he should've picked one of his other disguises: the *Playboy* photographer; the mule tanner circa 1860; even the ATM. So many perfect choices. Such was the pain of a master.

"I didn't mean—"

"Shut up," he snapped. Without another word, he kneeled down below the desk. From Devin's view, it looked and sounded as if he was rifling through a bag or a briefcase. A zipper purred. Leather stretched. Metal tools clicked against each other.

The moment he stood up, Devin saw the object of his

desire—a classic Swingline stapler. Sometimes the simple
ways were the best.

"Oh, God . . . ," Devin gasped. "What're you—?"

"Shut up," he repeated. Turning away from Devin, he
reached back into his bag, grabbed a box of staples, and
loaded the Swingline.

Unsure of what to say, Devin just stayed quiet. Better
to take advantage of the moment. With a deep breath,
she silently checked the strength of her bonds. She pulled
as hard as she could, but the handcuffs wouldn't give.

"They're eighty percent steel," the tall man warned,
brushing his hair behind his ear and slowly turning to
face her. "You're not going anywhere." As calm as a
yawn, he leaned toward Devin, his stomach slithering
against the top of the desk. She was stuck in the chair,
pushing back to get away from him. He was six inches
away from her face. "Ask me who I am," the man
growled.

"I already d—"

"*Why aren't you listening to me?*" he shouted, his hot
breath wisping against her features. Pouncing forward, he
reached out, grabbed her by the back of her neck, and
yanked her even closer. She turned her head to the side,
struggling to pull away, but the man just squeezed her neck
harder. "When you were little, Ms. McGee, did anyone
ever try stapling your skin to your collarbone?" With his
free hand, he opened the stapler to its full 180-degree position. "It's one of the few spots in the human body where
the bone is right there—though now that I think about
it, there's also the skull and the forehead . . ." Out of
the corner of her eye, she saw him raise the stapler toward
her face.

"Please . . . I promise—"

"You know the magic words, Ms. McGee."

"Okay, okay," she pleaded. "Please—tell me who you are."

Without warning, he released her neck, letting her collapse backward. Easing into his own seat, he made sure she was still watching. With his chin, he motioned to the small name tag pinned to his shirt. In thin black letters was the name FRAN.

"O-okay, *Fran,* what do you want?"

The tall Foot Locker employee nodded proudly and crossed one leg over the other. The perfect disguise. Back in control. "Like I told you, Ms. McGee, I just want to keep things fair."

"What do you mean *fair?*"

"Y'know, this whole Hightower fiasco."

"So this has something to do with Julia?"

The tall man uncrossed his legs, then crossed them the other way. "Have you ever seen a dog the first time it rides in a car?" he asked.

"What're you—"

"Just answer the question, Ms. McGee. Have you ever seen a—"

"No—not that I can remember."

"It's an incredible sight, really. The dog'll run around in the back, thinking everything's fine, and as the car actually starts moving, there'll be nothing out of the ordinary. Then, a block or two away, there'll come a point where the driver eventually has to slow down. When he hits the brakes, the dog's whole world comes undone. Y'see, as higher-ordered thinkers, we humans know to brace ourselves against momentum. That's what keeps us from smacking our faces on the windshield. That and seat belts. But dogs—when it's their first time in a car—

dogs can't grasp the concept of momentum. They don't know how to brace themselves. So they inevitably spend their first car ride falling to the floor every time the driver hits the brakes. Either that or they get sick all over the place. Or both."

"I don't understand."

"Pretend you're a dog, Ms. McGee. One day, your entire world is flat and unshakable; the next day, you go for a simple trip and you find out that not only is the world far more complex than you thought—but more important—if you don't brace yourself, the whole she-bang is going to rage out of your control."

"Are you threatening me?"

"If I were, you'd already be screaming." He squeezed the neck of the stapler and launched a single staple onto the desk. It hit with a ping. "It's a strange world, Ms. McGee. I'm just here to tell you that there's more to it than you know."

"So you're saying Julia's innocent?"

"No one's innocent. Not really."

"But . . . but—"

"Goats butt, birds fly, and children who are going on an outing with their father must get a good night's sleep." He grinned wide, proud of the *Mary Poppins* reference.

"Do you always find answers in children's entertainment?" Devin asked.

"Talk to the reporter. He's obsessed with *This Little Piggy Went to Market* . . ."

"What're you talking about? What reporter?"

"Patrick Roswell—at the *Gazette*. I think you two should get together. You've got a lot in common."

"I don't underst—"

"Think about it, Ms. McGee. Not everyone wants you to lose." Watching her with his hollow eyes, he let his words sink in. Then, in one quick movement, he hopped out of his seat and headed for the door.

"Wait a minute—how'm I gonna get out of here?"

"Oh, that's right. I almost forgot." Stopping in mid-step, he reached into his pocket, pulled out a tiny hand-cuff key, and moved back toward Devin. He leaned in close and pinched her cheeks.

"What're you—"

Before she could get the words out, he stuffed the key in her mouth.

"It'll take you a while to lean down and twist them open, but old man Houdini never seemed to mind. Nice meeting you, Ms. McGee."

As the tall man left the office, Devin pulled her right arm up and lowered her head to the now-extended hand-cuffs. Angling the key around in her mouth, she could feel the rust scraping against her teeth. When it finally peeked through her lips, it took less than thirty seconds to get it into the lock. The turning was the hard part. But when it eventually clicked, when the cuffs around her right wrist sprang open, she pulled her arm free and opened the other.

Shooting out of her seat, she ran for the door. If the elevator behaved as usual, she might still catch him. "Fran!" she shouted as she burst into the hallway. Running full speed, she dashed toward the elevator. But as she turned the final corner, she realized it was too late. The hall was empty. Fran was gone.

*   *   *

"HERE!" SISSY SHOUTED to the cab driver. "Stop the car!"

The cab screeched to a halt, sending Sissy slightly forward in her seat. "Haven't you ever heard of easing to a stop?" she barked.

The driver ignored the question. "Nine-fifty," he announced, pointing to the meter.

Sissy pulled out a ten-dollar bill and handed it to him.

"You want change?" he asked sarcastically.

"Actually, now I do." She put her hand out, waiting for the two quarters. No tips for smart-asses. When she got out of the car, she crossed in front of the cab and shot a final look at the driver. She then slapped her open palm against the hood of the cab, leaving the fifty cents sitting there.

Squinting his eyes, the driver slammed the gas and the cab peeled forward, just inches from sideswiping Sissy. Her skirt blew through the air, but she didn't bat an eye or even turn around. Small fish weren't worth it.

When she reached the curb, she looked up at the pink neon sign for Beats Me, her favorite store in the Village. With a quick look over her shoulder, she pulled open the oak-and-glass door, where a light jingle of holiday bells signaled her arrival.

Inside, the long rectangular room had four mannequins—one in each corner—all of them dressed like Cher, complete with monster hair. Two wore fishnets and skimpy black corsets, one wore a leather bikini with silver-linked chains around her stomach, and one was dressed like a nurse with a black leather mask that could barely contain all the thick black hair.

"Hiya, dear," a sweet voice that was all peaches said

from behind one of the many glass display cases. Looking up, Sissy saw a small old woman with silver-gray hair
that was pinned up in a tightly wrapped bun. With her
simple black cardigan, her understated orthopedic shoes,
and the reading glasses that dangled around her neck,
she wasn't a typical customer. She was the owner.

"Hey, Dottie," Sissy called out as she passed a display
case marked TONGUE-PICKABLE LOCKS. Heading straight
for an open bookcase on the lefthand wall, Sissy didn't
bother with small talk. She was already running late and
her associate would be here any minute. Still, Sissy was a
purist, which meant she couldn't pass up a quick look at
the Employee's Picks of the Week. Collected under a
handwritten sign marked NANA'S RAGING ORGASMS, the
featured items weren't only obsessively dangerous—they
were twenty percent off.

A scan of the items left her completely underwhelmed
and made her wonder for the first time if Dottie was
losing her edge.

"Anything you like?" Dottie called out.

"Not really."

Dottie's eyes went dark and her shoulders pitched with
irritation. "Don't give me that pity look, you bony little
psychopath!"

"Who're you calling bony, you has-been witch's tit."

"Preppie-lover."

"Diaper-wearer."

"Sock-sniffer."

"Gray-hairer."

"That's it!" Dottie shouted. "Enough with the old
jokes, you Barbie-doll bitch! You let another one get
loose, I'll put a boot in your eye faster than you can say
'Harder.' "

Yeeaaaah. Sissy grinned, wiping her lips with the back of her hand. Nothing like coming home.

Over her shoulder, the holiday bells jingled and the two old friends realized they were no longer alone. Turning around, Sissy assumed that her associate had finally arrived. The store wasn't the best meeting place, but Dottie was well known for her discretion. Sissy glanced down at her watch, then finally looked up to see who'd stepped inside. Her mouth dropped open and the blood drained from her face.

"Oh, God," Sissy blurted as her features went white. "What the hell're you doing here?"

CHAPTER

6

SISSY STARED IN wide-eyed terror as Luke Harrison shut the glass door of the Beats Me boutique with his heel, and pulled the shade down with his hook.

"Just what the fuck do you think you're doing?" Dottie asked.

"You're closed," Harrison said.

"The hell I am."

Dottie rushed him, flailing at his face. Harrison parried her smoothly with his steel limb and, with the quickness of a striking rattler, latched on to her throat with his hand.

"Harrison, don't hurt her!" Sissy screamed.

Harrison, dressed in a black suit, black turtleneck, and black wing tips, fixed the shop owner with a stiletto-like stare, then slowly let her go. He was a six-footer, lean and wiry as a coiled spring. His dark eyes, shaded by the

brim of his black fedora, looked like chips of burn-
ing coal.

"Take a hike, old woman," he said to Dottie.

"What?"

"Dottie, do as he says," Sissy pleaded. "Come back in
half an hour. I'll watch the place."

Dottie straightened her bun and backed toward the
door, never taking her eyes off Harrison.

"Call me an old lady again and you'll be searching the
sewers for your nuts," she said. "Sissy, you want me to
call the cops?"

"Dottie, he *is* a cop."

"I could tell," Dottie said. She slammed the door behind her.

"Jesus, Harrison, you didn't have to manhandle her,"
Sissy said.

"Get in the back room. You have some explaining
to do."

"Hey, easy does it, Lukey-Wookey," she cooed, thrusting her perfect breasts toward him. "Dottie has a bed
back there. Why don't we take advantage of it? You
can learn firsthand what makes me so valuable to the
Organization."

Harrison shoved her roughly through the beaded cur-
tain into the back room.

"If it turns out you've been playing both ends against
the middle," he said, "the only organization you'll be
valuable to is the International Brotherhood of Cemetery
Worms."

Sissy faced him defiantly. "I don't know what you're
talking about," she said with conviction.

"I'm talking about a hand belonging to Arthur Hightower's lawyer that was just delivered to Rob Rutledge

in a box. That sound like anyone's technique you know of?" He shook his hook at her for emphasis.

"Stefan is involved in this?" she asked incredulously. "I thought he was dead."

"On the contrary. He's still happily making other people dead, most recently, I suspect, Attorney Joe Kellogg."

Everyone in the Organization—the O, as most referred to it—knew that Stefan Ghorse had severed Harrison's left hand, and then tied a tourniquet around the stump, allowing the agent to live to face the humiliation of having been trapped, then maimed, by his quarry. Harrison, a legend for his toughness and uncompromising honesty, had vowed to get even, but five years had passed, and Stefan was still in the dissection business.

The O was a highly secret collaboration with murky origins and financing. Only a few select operatives even knew it existed. The initial goal of the O was to stop international terrorists functioning around the world. Over the years since its creation, though, the group had extended its range to include large-scale narcotics traffickers, arms dealers, and now, those who would foment international financial chaos.

"Kellogg was a jerk," Sissy said. "He made a pass at me the first time he met me."

"You should have taken him up on his offer. I suspect he was one of the very few who knew what Rutledge and Hightower were up to."

"I was dating his boss's son, for chrissakes. Talk about disloyal."

"Sissy, as far as I'm concerned, you define the word."

"Up yours, Harrison. I've always done whatever those buffoons running the O have asked of me."

"And then some. You were just supposed to date Morgan Hightower to get close to his old man—not to *marry* him."

Sissy favored him with another coy smile and fingered the two-carat ruby pendant suspended over her spectacular cleavage.

"He made me an offer I couldn't refuse."

Harrison's ebony eyes flashed.

"The security and stability of the world as we know it is hanging by a thread, and all you can think of is adding to your jewelry collection. What a gal. Now, what do you know about Kellogg? Was he Hightower and Rutledge's point man?"

"Kellogg's a pretentious fop with more weaknesses than a Yugo. If they made someone that vulnerable their point man, they're not bright enough to pull off anything this big. Kellogg may have known some parts of their plan, but I seriously doubt he knew everything."

"Well, that hand tells me that whatever Kellogg knew, Stefan and his employers know, too."

"Such brutes. If they had half a brain, they would have known that a pair of talented lips in just the right spot would have gotten more out of Kellogg than any oversized, cross-dressing torture master ever could."

Without warning, Harrison brought his hook up under Sissy's chin, forcing her onto her tiptoes.

"Sissy, mark my words," he said through clenched teeth. "If I learn that you're holding out on us, you're going to need prostheses in places they haven't invented them for."

He lowered the hook and brushed the curved edge up her crotch. Then he whirled and stormed from the shop.

Shaken, Sissy sank to the corner of the bed. His loss to

Stefan Ghorse aside, Harrison was as brilliant, tough, and determined as anyone in the agency—most definitely someone to be careful of, and if necessary, to be dealt with. It was several minutes before she felt able to stand. As she did, there was a firm knock on the alley door behind her.

"Yes?" she said.

"It's me."

Sissy opened the door a crack, then all the way.

"Where in the hell were you when I needed you?" she said.

IT'S A STRANGE world, Ms. McGee . . . There's more to it than you know . . . Talk to the reporter . . . Patrick Roswell . . . I think you two should get together . . . Not everyone wants you to lose . . .

Devin propped her feet up on her desk and replayed the bizarre exchange with the even more bizarre Fran. The Hightower case had been strange from the beginning. With limitless piles of money at her disposal, and a case against her that was hardly open and shut, Julia had eschewed the high-powered firms in favor of a young solo practitioner with a limited, albeit reasonably impressive, record as a criminal attorney.

Why?

Julia had never told Devin the reason she had been chosen as her defense counsel, but subsequently, Joe Kellogg, the Hightower family's attorney, took credit for recommending her. Never taking his eyes off her breasts, he had praised her work on behalf of the son of a friend of his, whom Devin had gotten cleared of an assault charge. In fact, she had put together a rather brilliant defense for the kid, but enough to justify placing a billion-aire's wife in her hands? Extremely doubtful.

Why?

Now, with the case against Julia still riding a motive/method/opportunity high, she was being told by a gigantic wacko with a blond wig that there was more to this case than she knew, and that Julia's survival might depend on a reporter named Roswell.

"What in the hell is going on?" Devin said out loud.

Retrieving the phone book from the shelf across her office would have meant taking her feet off her desk and thus leaving her favorite comfort zone. Instead, she pulled the phone over by the cord and dialed information. Why not? she thought as she wrote down the number of the *Gazette*. With a $20,000 retainer in the bank, she could afford to run up telephone expenses like the big boys.

"The *Gazette*, may I help you?" the receptionist asked, her accent heavy Brooklyn. Devin thought she could hear the woman snapping her gum.

"I'm trying to locate a reporter named Patrick Roswell," she said.

"We got a Patrick Roswell working here, ma'am, but he ain't no reporter. He's in sales."

"Sales?"

"You know, advertising."

Devin lowered her feet to the floor.

"He sells advertising?"

"That's what I said."

"Why did Wacko say he was a reporter?" Devin thought out loud.

"What?"

"Oh, sorry. Could I speak to Mr. Roswell, please?"

"If he was here, you probably could."

Devin wanted to reach through the phone and rip out the receptionist's tongue. Surly, ill-spoken, and snapping gum—the perfect company spokeswoman.

"My name's Devin McGee. I'd like to leave my number for Mr. Roswell and have him call me back."

"He's got voice mail. Dial back and punch in extension two-two-seven-four instead of 'O' like you did."

"Can't you connect me?"

"Nope."

Jerk, Devin thought.

"Well thanks a million anyway," she said.

"Wait a minute. Devin McGee. You that Hightower lady's lawyer?"

"I am, yes."

"Well I been watchin' the case on Court TV every chance I get. You're doing a great job. Keep up the good work."

"Why, thank you," Devin said, genuinely flattered, and now placing the receptionist closer to Marie Curie than to jerk.

"I still think she done it, though," the woman said. Then she hung up.

Devin listened to the dial tone for half a minute, after which she called Patrick Roswell's line and left a message on his voice mail.

Not everyone wants you to lose. . . .

Devin pictured her Toyota being blown to smithereens. Not everyone wanted her to live, either.

There's more to it than you know. . . .

"You got it right there, Fran," Devin said.

She emptied the contents of the thick Hightower file

onto her desk and flipped through it for the hundredth time. Nothing new leapt out at her.

More than you know . . .

Devin snatched up the phone and dialed the Hightower mansion. Julia was there, and clearly well into her cups. Devin knew she might be doing a farewell fandango on her high-profile, $20,000 case, but she needed some answers that only her inebriated client could provide.

"Have some black coffee, Julia," she said. "I'm coming out to ask you some questions. . . . No, no, Julia, I'm going to drive my rental car out there and ask you some questions. So go take an ice-cold shower. Because if you can't or won't deal with me straight, it's find another lawyer."

JACK POWELL USED a toothbrush to scrub out the corners of the meat slicer, even though the machine was, as was everything else in the little restaurant, spotless. He was a neatness freak to the point where even Janie got annoyed with him sometimes, but he knew that nothing could shut a place like theirs down quicker than a mouse, or a roach, or even some scum on a knife. He was a black man operating an eatery in a predominantly white neighborhood. There were people anxious to see their place go under. Well, it wasn't going to happen. Even though the restaurant was still struggling, even though he was on the phone with loan people almost weekly asking for a little more time, it wasn't going to happen. His mother had emptied what was left of her bank account to help them get started. Now, with the baby on the way, there was no chance they could pay her back in the foreseeable future—at least there wasn't before he got the notice calling him to jury duty.

Julia Hightower. When Jack realized that he was being examined to sit on her jury, his heart almost stopped. What justice. What luck! He had answered the attorneys' questions with the care he gave to keeping his restaurant clean. When he learned he had been selected as one of the twelve, he nearly let out a whoop of joy.

"You all right, Jack?" Janie asked.

Startled, Jack looked across to where his pregnant wife was arranging the napkin holders and condiments just so on each table.

"Huh? Oh, sure," he said, "I'm fine. Just lost in thought."

"About the trial?"

"No," he lied, "about the baby. Listen, hon, I'm going to go for a walk to clear my head."

"Want company?"

"Maybe later. I'll be back in half an hour. Want anything? Ice cream? Pickles?"

"No, no. I'm fine."

She came over, put her arms around him, and nestled her head against his chest. He buried his face in her hair. She smelled so perfect, so clean.

"We're gonna have a wonderful baby," he whispered. "And she's gonna have the best mom in the world. I'll be back in a little while."

He released her gently and headed toward the door.

"Jack?"

"Yes?"

"You sure everything's okay?"

"Honey, things couldn't be better. Trust me on that."

He took another step.

"Jack?"

"Yes?"

"Have you heard anything from that man with . . . with the missing toe?"

"Nope. I hope we do, though. He's wearing some of my clothes."

"Why do you think he didn't want to go to the hospital?"

"No idea. Maybe he's just scared of doctors."

"Maybe so. The way that toe was sliced off looked like he had just seen one."

Powell chuckled at the thought.

"You go on back and put your feet up, Janie. I'll stop by the deli on the way back and bring you some of that halvah you like so much."

Jack walked three blocks before picking out a pay phone. Janie loved walking, and this was not the time to have her catch up with him. As he dialed, he pictured his mother in her two-room apartment on One-eighteenth, tidying up as always. He also imagined his older brother Marshall twitching and grimacing in his wheelchair, watching some mindless cartoons, or worse, some lousy talk show. Marshall was an absolute dear, but his limited IQ and limiting cerebral palsy made the future elements of his life a certainty—home care until his mother couldn't handle it anymore, then an institution.

"Hey, Ma, what's happenin'?" Jack said.

"Jackie, what's all that traffic noise? You callin' me from a pay phone? Is everything all right? Janie? The baby?"

"Everything's fine, Ma. How's Marshall doing?"

"Same as ever. He's been watchin' *The Beverly Hill-billies*. I really think that's his favorite show."

Jack shook his head sadly. Mother Teresa could have taken lessons from Loretta Powell. A brain-damaged child out of wedlock at age fifteen. Twin boys also out of wedlock two years later. Eventually, Loretta had pulled herself together, finished high school, and even a medical assistant's course. The state offered some help for her debilitated child, but they demanded he be institutionalized to get it. Loretta would have none of that. There was some money—from Marshall's father, she said. But that account was empty now. Loretta and Marshall lived off her part-time job as receptionist in a doctor's office, small checks from Jack when he could, and once in a while, even a little from his twin brother, Wyn. Wyn Powell had tried and lost as a professional boxer, and was fortunate to have gotten out of the ring with his brain mostly intact. Now he worked as an equipment man in one of Harlem's smelliest gyms, and as a corner man for the dregs of the sport.

"You're doing a great job with him, Ma," Jack said.

"Why shouldn't I? He's my son. Speaking of which, have you heard from Wyn?"

"Not for a week or so. But I think everything's fine with him."

"I wish he'd get married. Find someone like your Janie."

"He will, Ma. You need anything?"

"Just for you and Janie and Wyn to be well."

"Take care, Ma. We'll be by later in the week."

"Good-bye, son."

Loretta had never talked about Jack's and Wyn's father except to say that he was a kind man who needed to find himself. She never spoke of Marshall's father, either, but as Jack grew older, it was clear to him that whoever it was, he was white. The man's identity had remained Loretta's secret for nearly twenty-five years. Then, home on leave and searching a bottom dresser drawer for his birth certificate, Jack had stumbled on the letter.

Jack dropped in another quarter and dialed the gym.

"Wyn, what's the deal?" he asked when his twin was finally brought to the phone.

"I can't get ahold of him."

"Whaddaya mean? He's got an office, doesn't he?"

"Yeah, but they keep telling me he's not in."

"You leave your name?"

"Of course I left my name. I told him I was callin' about Loretta Powell, just like you said to."

"Damn it, Wyn. We've got to talk to him. He's the one who sent that letter. He's the one who's going to come up with the money. Keep callin' him."

"I will. I will."

"Ma needs that money. So does Marshall. And damn it, Wyn, so do we."

Years before, when he found the letter, Jack had called the lawyer who wrote it and demanded money for his mother. Joe Kellogg had simply laughed.

"We got papers, son," he had said. "Papers signed by your mother after she turned twenty-one. Papers that'll stand up in any court. We sent Loretta money for twenty years, and she's not getting another cent."

Jack had pushed matters, claiming that whatever she was sent wasn't nearly enough, but Kellogg wouldn't budge.

"Don't you dare try to shake me down, son," he warned.

When Jack persisted, Kellogg apparently contacted

Loretta. Jack would never know what the lawyer had said to his mother, but he knew fear in the woman when he saw it. And when she demanded that he let the whole matter drop, Loretta Powell was scared stiff.

Jack encouraged Wyn to keep trying. Then he slammed the receiver down. The letter hadn't said as much, and Loretta absolutely refused to speak of the matter, but in time Jack had deduced that Arthur Hightower had to be Marshall's father. At his mother's insistence, he had let the matter drop, at least for the time being. Then, with Hightower's murder and subsequent cremation, it seemed that all hope had died. But now, the weapon of justice and retribution had been placed in his hands—a jury summons.

McGINTY'S MEATS WAS a vast, single-story warehouse on the river side of the West Side Highway, not far from the permanently docked aircraft carrier *Intrepid*. Patrick paid off the cabbie and approached the south-side entrance as the giant clown had instructed. His foot was throbbing, but the notion that soon it might be whole again dampened some of the pain. In a short while, after he had helped the police find Kellogg's body in meat locker three, he would go to a specific alley on West Sixtieth between Seventh and Eighth, and find his toe in a cooler behind some barrels. He would then be off to the Hospital of Bone and Joint Surgery for replantation.

The huge clown's instructions had been quite specific, including the description Patrick was to give the police of the man who had tortured him and tipped him off about Kellogg's body. If he tried any shortcuts or double crosses, he would be revisited by his grease-painted nemesis and divested of another, far more essential body part.

For nearly ten minutes Patrick stood outside the door on the loading dock shivering against a harsh wind. He had been warned not to go inside until the police arrived. Finally he heard the sirens approaching. Moments later an unmarked sedan and a cruiser pulled up. A rumpled, cadaverous man wearing a fur-lined parka introduced himself as Detective Guttman.

"I understand you know where I can find the rest of Joe Kellogg," he said.

Patrick shivered from a sudden chill that had nothing to do with meteorology.

"The rest?" he asked.

"Yeah," Guttman replied. "What we have so far is his right hand. It was delivered in a box to Robert Rutledge, the Wall Street money man. Kellogg's prints popped up because of a driving-under arrest he had a few years ago. Now, where's the body?"

"My—um—source said it was in meat locker three," he said.

Guttman opened the door to the warehouse and stepped inside. There seemed to be no one around.

"See if you can find someone," he ordered one of the uniformed cops. "You been in here yet?" he asked Patrick.

"No."

"Why're you limping?"

"A man drugged me in a bar, then cut off my toe."

"Oh," Guttman said matter-of-factly, clearly jaded by his years with the NYPD. "Where did he do that, here?"

"I don't know where, but it wasn't here."

"And he gave you the tip about Kellogg's body?"

"He did."

"Why would he do that?"

"I don't know. Detective, could we get on down to locker three? My foot is killing me."

"Why do you think this guy just took your toe, and not your hand like Kellogg?"

"I have no idea."

"You know Robert Rutledge?"

"I've heard of him. That's all." Patrick flashed on his toe sitting in a Playmate Cooler behind some trash barrels on West Sixtieth. "Please," he begged.

"Okay, let's go see what you've got."

At that moment, John Whitechapel burst through the door behind them with a rotund photographer named Dave Salazar. Patrick made clumsy introductions. Guttman acted as if he couldn't care less about the newspaper editor, but he gave strict instructions to the photographer to shoot only what Guttman told him to shoot. The three newsmen and two remaining policemen stood back as Guttman shoved open the door to locker three. They walked down the rows of chilled meat carcasses, then back. Nothing.

"You sure it was room three?" Guttman asked.

"That's what he said."

They checked the other two cold rooms. Nothing. The uniformed cop returned with the manager of McGinty's, a short balding man who stuttered badly. The man stammered that he was never away from the warehouse during business hours, and had seen nothing suspicious over the past two days.

Guttman took the manager's news and the absence of the promised corpus delicti in stride, but John Whitechapel was livid.

"This is the last straw, Roswell," he blustered. "As of this moment, you're suspended from the paper until you present me with a letter from a bona fide psychiatrist certifying that you're sane. And if any shrink does give you one, I'll want a letter from *his* shrink certifying *he's* sane!"

Without waiting for a response, he grabbed his photographer by the arm and dragged him from McGinty's.

"Tsk, tsk," Guttman said. "There goes one unhappy camper." He led his entourage out to their cars. "Roswell, I think you've got to come down to the station and answer some questions."

"I can't."

"Excuse me, but that's not a response we were taught to accept in the police academy."

"It's my toe. The guy who cut it off told me where the cooler is containing it. I've got to get it and have it sewn back on before it's too late."

"This guy, what did he look like?"

Patrick debated telling the truth or the lie he had been instructed by the clown to tell. He was being systematically destroyed by the man, he acknowledged, but this was hardly the time to be rebellious.

"I don't know his name," he said, "but he was about six feet tall, thin, and dressed all in black. He had a real narrow face and, oh yes, he had a hook instead of a hand."

"What?"

"A hook. His left hand was missing and instead he had one of those steel hooks. Now, can I please go?"

"Hands, toes, hooks," Guttman muttered. "This is really gonna be fun."

"Can I please go?" Patrick begged.

"Roswell, exactly when did this man with the hook cut off your toe?"

"I don't know. The last thing I remember before I was drugged was being in the Sweeney Hotel at seven."

"In the evening?"

"Yes."

"That's like sixteen hours ago."

"I suppose."

"I've got some bad news for you, Roswell. There's no way that toe is going back on your foot."

"What do you mean?"

"I mean surgeons rarely if ever replace *any* toes, especially the little piggy. And they certainly don't do it after sixteen hours. Six hours would be pushing it."

"How do you know that?" Patrick asked, stunned.

"I don't want to tell you how many body parts we cops get to rush to the hospital. I know all the rules about replantation. And the rules say you better get used to having nine toes. Just be grateful it wasn't the big one. That toe helps keep you balanced. The only thing the one you lost does is go wee wee wee all the way home. Now, how's about hopping into the back like a good little amputee, and we'll go to the station for a chat."

PATRICK LOCATED THE number for Hammer, Crain & Rutledge, and called from a pay phone in the lobby of the precinct house. He had taken more than enough abuse from everybody. Now, damn it, he was going to fight back. On the way from McGinty's to the station, Guttman had driven him into the alley on West Sixtieth. There was a small cooler behind the barrels right where it was supposed to be, but instead of his toe, all that was inside was a red, rubber clown's nose.

All it took to get Robert Rutledge on the phone was the mention of a single name: Joe Kellogg. Two minutes later, Patrick was in a cab headed downtown. Despite the physical and emotional abuse he had suffered at the hands of the mammoth clown, he did not choose to further erode his credibility by recanting the description he had given Guttman of his assailant.

"Sounds like sort of a cross between *Men in Black* and *The Fugitive*," was all the detective said.

Patrick was not by nature a violent man, but he felt he had been pushed over the edge. No job, no allies, no toe—and no place to go but up. He felt capable of almost anything. He was going to get to the bottom of the High-tower murder and wreak some measure of vengeance on the clown, or he was going to die trying.

The cab dropped him off outside the gleaming World Financial Center. The security guard in the lobby was expecting him and escorted him across the polished marble to the elevators.

"The button's marked," he said. "Turn left when you get out. The office staff has gone for the day, but Mr. Rutledge is expecting you."

Patrick thanked the man. It felt good to be treated with some respect.

Robert Rutledge seemed like the logical starting point in Patrick's counterattack. Each of them had information to offer the other. Patrick knew something of the man who had sent Rutledge the hand. And with luck, the financier would know why. It wasn't much, but it was a start.

Patrick stepped off the elevator into an office more

opulent than anything he had ever seen. He turned left and headed down a long, broad corridor lined with millions of dollars in French impressionist art. No prints. Rutledge was in his office at the very end of the hallway—a little man, standing with his back to Patrick, gazing out at the city.

"Welcome, Mr. Roswell," he said, turning slowly.

Patrick stood in the doorway staring at the tycoon, absolutely stunned.

"Thank you for seeing me so quickly," he managed.

"Is something the matter?" Rutledge asked. "You're looking at me very queerly."

"Oh no, nothing's the matter. I've never been in a place quite like this. That's all."

Patrick tried to divert his gaze from the man, but with only marginal success. It was astounding. Remarkable. Incredible. Robert Rutledge, one of the wealthiest, most powerful men in the world was an absolute dead ringer for Henry Cloutier, the crossword-challenged night watchman at Miller Tool and Die.

CHAPTER

7

JULIA HIGHTOWER LEANED toward her dressing table mirror and stared at the ruin that was her face. Red-veined eyes, pouches like IV bags beneath them, dewlaps that hung from her jaws and flapped in the breeze like a bloodhound's, and overlaying all of it a spiderweb of lines and creases like the embalming muslin wrapped over a desiccated mummy. Only fifty-five years old and she looked eighty. So much for the lifestyle of the rich and shameless. She'd consulted the best plastic surgeons, skin-care specialists, and mind-over-body transcendentalists in the world, and not one of them could save her from this face—er, fate.

She rose from her dressing table and turned to survey the ruin that was her life. No—not ruin, for that implied that something worthwhile once existed here. Wasteland—that was the word for it. Her life was an utter wasteland of idleness and boredom and the misery

139

that came from never having done anything useful on this earth. The only honest work she ever did was at the Buckshot Cafe in Salt Gully, Texas, when she was eighteen years old and worked that many hours every day, slinging hash to a motley assortment of wildcatters who were all trying their luck in the oil fields. Her back ached and her feet swelled and she had the time of her life trading jokes, scraping tips off the counter, and flirting with every man who swung through the door.

She could've married any of them, but Arthur Hightower was the one whose well came in first. She could still remember the day he burst through that door with a grin like a big white crescent moon gleaming out of his oil-blackened face. "I did it!" he'd roared, then grabbed Julia and swung her in a wild twirl through the cafe. Both of them were laughing so breathlessly that it was five minutes before he could propose and she could accept. But accept she did. It didn't matter that she didn't love him. All that mattered was that he'd struck oil, and that she'd struck him.

Julia came from a generation of women who thought it was a perfectly worthy ambition to marry money and then retire. (Oh, who was she kidding? Every generation of women thought that, including today's bright young lovelies who held advanced degrees and still spent every spare moment at the golf/yacht/country club casting about for a likely millionaire.) Now, thirty-eight years too late, Julia knew better. The only money that mattered was the money you earned yourself. Married money, even inherited money, counted for nothing in this world; it was only numbers written in disappearing ink on disintegrating paper. And while anyone could lose their fortune—she had dozens of former friends who were former millionaires gone bust—the difference was that even after their money was gone, they still had the accomplishment of having earned it. They had still done something that counted for something, if only for a moment. Whereas all she'd done was marry Arthur and give birth to two children under heavy sedation. She'd conceived them under sedation, too, now that she thought of it, which might explain why they were the two most dull and indifferent people she'd ever had the displeasure of knowing.

She drifted across the Aubusson rug of her boudoir to stand—sway—at the window and watch the sun sink into the night. Devin McGee was on her way over to ask her some questions, she had said. But Julia had already answered all the obvious ones:

1. Did you kill your husband?

No. At least, I don't think so. And if I did, it couldn't have been between November second and November ninth, because I spent that week at a New Age detox spa and tennis clinic in the Berkshires, and although the "tox" didn't quite "de," I did have a lovely seaweed wrap and the most invigorating high colonic purge.

2. Who else had a key to the freezer?

I don't know, but my key was on the household ring for three years, and anyone could have used it or had a copy made.

No, Devin knew all that. The question that was driving her out here this evening had to be the one she was too insecure to ask before—*Why did you hire me?*—and that was the one question Julia refused to answer.

She turned away from the window and went into her closet and wandered its many aisles in search of an appropriate outfit for the evening. Here were her golfing plaids and her sailing whites, over here her evening gowns, her luncheon suits, and her at-home ensembles. She reached a cul-de-sac in the closet and selected a not-at-home ensemble. For that was what she planned to be when Devin arrived—not at home. Julia had suffered enough humiliation of late. She would not be compelled to endure any more tonight by telling Devin the circumstances of how they first met.

It happened one night twenty-five years ago when Julia jolted awake on a city bus without a clue of how she'd gotten there. Also without her purse, her jewelry, and one of her Ferragamo pumps. The bus was empty; the driver was returning to the terminal at the end of his route. In a panic—well, it was her first major bender; she wasn't yet proficient at it—she'd lurched to her feet. Instantly she regretted it. The next thing she knew she was hanging over a pool of vomit and the driver was speaking to her in a soft and soothing voice. He helped her to a phone and dialed the number she mumbled at him, and when no one answered, he took a deep breath and drove her to his own house in Queens. His wife spoke softly, too, as she made a pot of coffee and sponged the stains off Julia's cashmere sweater, and all the while a solemn little girl in a pink nightgown crouched on the stairs and peeked wide-eyed through the balustrades—until at last Julia recalled the actual digits of her telephone number and the chauffeur arrived dutifully if doubtfully to take her home.

She never mentioned the incident to anyone and certainly never had any further contact with the bus driver or his wife. But over the years she'd set aside enough of her pin money to establish an anonymous scholarship fund that paid their little girl's tuition through college and law school. It was meant to be a grand and glamorous gesture, something to smile secretively about when Devin was appointed to the Supreme Court, for example. Certainly Julia never planned to extract any quid pro quo. But when the sky fell in and the police arrived to arrest her for Arthur's murder, all she could think of was her long-ago dependence on the kindness of strangers, and she called Devin McGee.

She finished dressing and hurried down the stairs with her everyday mink draped over her shoulders. She would not be home when Devin arrived; she would not be interrogated about any of this. Devin might withdraw from the case, Julia might be convicted—heavens, she might even be executed—but far better any of those scenarios than the one in which she, Julia Conners Hightower, was reduced to the pathetic admission that the only people who were ever kind to her were a transit worker and his wife.

She left the mansion through the conservatory door and headed for the ten-car garage at the base of the hill. Twilight was falling along with the temperature, and Julia shivered as she plowed through last night's snowfall to the side entrance of the garage. She stepped inside and reached for the light switch as someone reached for her.

A rancid-smelling hand clamped over her mouth, and an arm like a side of beef swung across her chest and squeezed up high against her throat. A voice rasped in her ear: "You make a sound, it'll be your last, you hear me?"

There was a faint involuntary gurgling in her throat, but she nodded. The man behind her felt hard and massive, and he stank of a fermented brew of sweat, Ben-Gay, and—was that?—yes, Dr. Scholl's foot spray.

"You know who I am?" he growled.

She shook her head emphatically.

"Picture the courtroom, and now picture the jury box." He eased his clammy hand from her mouth, but his arm remained soldered to her collarbone. "I'm juror number five."

"The retired home ec teacher?" Julia said doubtfully.

"No! I mean—number six."

"The pregnant cashier?" she exclaimed.

"Number seven then," he snapped. "Jeez."

"Ohh," she breathed as the image came to her. "The paramedic turned sandwich shop owner?"

"Yeah," he said happily. "That's me."

"Why are you here? What do you want?"

"Nothin' you can't spare. Say half a mill."

"I beg your pardon?"

"Half a million dollars. Cash. Or I get that jury to convict your lily-white ass. Don't you think I can't do it either. I can be a pretty persuasive guy when I wanna." He tightened his arm against her windpipe.

"Oh, but I couldn't possibly—" she squeaked.

"Don't give me that, lady. You got more than that in jewelry layin' around the house."

"Fine. Then take the jewelry."

"And get nailed the first time I try to sell any of it? No way. You sell it if you have to. I want cash."

"But that takes time—"

"You got until the jury goes into deliberations. If I have half a mill in cash in my pocket, I'll do my best to get you off. If I don't, then that jury's gonna vote unanimously to convict you. I guarantee it."

"I see," Julia murmured after a moment. "And how will I find you to give you the cash?"

"I'll find you. Don't worry."

He made her lie facedown on the concrete floor—a disgusting surface, she thought; why did they never install carpeting here?—until he left, and when she finally pulled herself to her feet, the door was open and he'd disappeared into the night.

She leaned shakily against the fender of Morgan's Maserati while she reviewed her options. She could report this threat to Judge Hardy, of course, but whom would he believe? A presumed murderess on trial for her life, or an honest citizen trying to do his civic duty for $8.45 a day? Another option was simply to pay him the half million, but Julia knew all about the never-ending circle of blackmail. One of her former millionaire, former friends was the victim of blackmail. His company had bribed a foreign official to gain a lucrative shipping contract, but too many people knew too much, and he paid out ten times more in extortion than he ever could have realized from the shipping contract. Eventually the company was bankrupt and he wound up teaching the fox-trot at an Arthur Murray studio in Paramus, New Jersey. And although he was reportedly happier than he'd ever been, Julia decided she'd rather not get sucked down that particular drain. Her fox-trot wasn't that good.

No, the only palatable option was the one that had been lurking in the back of her mind since Thanksgiving. Now was the moment. It was time to take her bow, bid her adieu, make her exit, *flee*.

She hurried back up the hill to pack a bag and make a phone call, then snowplowed back to the garage again. Who knew? she thought, backing her Bentley out of the bay. Life on the lam might be fun. It could be a glorious adventure to live in hiding. She looked in the rearview mirror and shuddered. At any rate, she'd never have to fret about the ruin of her face again.

PATRICK ROSWELL WAS being stonewalled.

"Joe Kellogg was our attorney," Robert Rutledge said gravely. He was on his feet behind his desk with the Manhattan skyline arrayed behind him, a deliberately dazzling display. "Though why I should be the recipient of that appalling package—" He spread his hands in helpless surrender to the vagaries of violence. "After all, isn't it enough that we lost our lawyer?"

"Wait," Patrick said. "I thought he was Arthur Hightower's lawyer."

"Was he?" Rutledge shrugged. "Well, I expect Joe had many other clients. He was free to do so, you know. An attorney-client relationship isn't like a marriage." He gave a worldly chuckle. "Or—perhaps it is."

Patrick laughed politely and drew closer to the little man. The resemblance was uncanny, but now he could see that that was all it was—a resemblance. The features were the same, but where Henry's were soft and dull, Rutledge's were sharp and bright.

"Was he working on some kind of deal for your company?" Patrick asked him.

Rutledge pursed his lips and shook his head regretfully. "I'd like to be able to answer your questions. Really. But that would be privileged information, and if I tell you, it's the same as telling the world. I am sorry."

Patrick gritted his teeth with frustration, not to mention pain. He shifted his weight to ease the pressure on his missing toe. "Can you at least tell me when you last saw him?"

"No harm there, I suppose. Let me see." Rutledge flipped through a few pages on his desk calendar. "Lunch last Wednesday." He looked up with a keen light behind his smile. "Meanwhile—you said something on the phone about information I'd find valuable?"

"What? Oh, right." Patrick decided to stonewall, too. If he wasn't going to get any information, he sure as hell wasn't going to give any. As an unemployed amputee, he had the right to be moody. "Actually, it's a stock tip."

"*You* have a stock tip for *me*?"

"Yep. Miller Tool and Die. Know it?"

Nothing registered on the man's face beyond astonishment at Patrick's audacity.

"Low tech. Trust me, it's the latest wave," Patrick said.

Rutledge stalked around his desk. "Young man—," he began in high dudgeon.

"I'll show myself out," Patrick said hastily, and closed the door as he left.

The neurons were screaming up and down his leg, but he found that it didn't hurt so much if he turned his foot to the inside as he put his weight on it. He hobbled that way across the wide expanse of the reception area toward the bank of elevators. Then abruptly he stopped, pivoted, and marched himself back to the desk outside Rutledge's office door.

He blinked. CORDELIA BAXTER, the nameplate read. Folded beside the blotter was today's *New York Times*. Turned to the crossword puzzle. Which was completed. In ink.

He hurried to the elevator, all pain forgotten, and as it

descended the floors, he reviewed the facts: Robert S. Rutledge, master of the universe, had a puzzle-loving assistant named Cordelia. Henry Cloutier, mild-mannered night watchman and dead ringer for Rutledge, had an unlikely fiancée, a beautiful, puzzle-loving woman named Cordelia, who took him to the Sweeney Hotel on the same night that Arthur Hightower happened to be a guest in the room next door. And finally, Joe Kellogg, attorney for Arthur Hightower and, perhaps, Robert Rutledge, was lured to that same Sweeney Hotel by a beautiful, puzzle-loving woman named Cordelia, and he hadn't been seen since. At least not in one piece.

"Coincidence?" Patrick said to himself as the doors opened on the lobby. "I think not."

He looked at his watch. It was six-thirty, and Henry's shift began at seven. A rush of adrenaline carried him out of the building, where he hailed a cab at the curb and jumped in, blurting the address for Miller Tool and Die.

Now the neurons were humming in his brain. He was on to something, he knew it. Cordelia was the glue that held this web together. She was the centerpiece of this mystery, the linchpin of these axles, the hub of all these spokes, the key to all these locks— A hundred clichés sprang to life as the story began to write itself in Patrick's mind. This was his big break. So what if he didn't have a job at the *Gazette*? He had a story! In fact, thank God he got fired, because now he was a free agent and could peddle his work to the highest bidder. He owed a debt of gratitude to John Whitechapel. When his story ran— page one, above the fold, in, say, the *Times*, or no! the *Post*—he'd send Whitechapel a bottle of cognac and let him stew in it.

The cab crossed into the factory district north of

Chelsea, and Patrick sat up straight and watchful. What was Cordelia's game? he wondered, already slipping into the parlance of a hard-eyed investigative journalist. Why did she latch on to Henry and take him to the Sweeney that night? Was she hoping to trick Hightower into thinking Henry was Rutledge? But what for? Patrick thought back to his barroom conversation with Joe Kellogg. Hightower missed an appointment on November third to sign papers they'd been working on for six months. The next day—no, wait, *that very night*— Arthur was in the Sweeney Hotel while Cordelia was next door with Henry. Did she somehow use Henry to trick Hightower into signing those papers?

Or did she arrange it so that Arthur would never sign another paper again? Could Cordelia be the killer?

Patrick's heart was racing by the time the cab pulled up to the darkened factory. He dug in his pocket for the fare and was starting to hand it over the seat when a small black coupe pulled to a stop on the other side of the street. He glanced at it as the passenger door opened and the dome light switched on inside. A beautiful, auburn-haired woman was behind the wheel, and her passenger was Henry Cloutier.

Patrick ducked down until his eyes were level with the bottom of the window. She had to be Cordelia. It was unlikely enough for Henry to have one such beauty in his life, let alone two.

"You gettin' out or what?" the cabbie said.

"Ssshh," Patrick explained.

It appeared that Henry and Cordelia were quarreling— or at least that she was. Her brows were knitted and she seemed to be biting out her words, while poor Henry was begging and pleading with his whipped-puppy eyes and his lower lip stuck out. Cordelia shook her head, and Henry begged some more; then she pointed to the door and he climbed out of the car with his head down and his shoulders shaking.

She must have cut him loose tonight, Patrick guessed. Whatever her game was, she had no further use for the little night watchman. His door was barely closed before she threw the car in gear and took off.

"Follow that car!" Patrick shouted.

It was something he'd always wanted to say, and the amazing thing was that the driver actually did it. He threw the cab into gear, squealed a U-turn across the street, and lit out after the little black coupe.

THE GATES WERE open when Devin arrived at Hightower Hill, and she drove the rented Taurus through them and up the twisting drive to the entrance court of the mansion. No one had shoveled the walk since last night, and the snow seeped in around the edges of her high-heeled pumps as she stormed to the front door and leaned on the bell. She could hear the chimes echoing inside, but no one answered. She pressed the bell again, then again, and finally resorted to hammering on the door, but there was still no answer.

She stood fuming on the doorstep while the snow melted and formed ice pools inside her shoes. She could believe that Julia was passed out drunk in there, but where were the servants? It must be true what they said: You really couldn't get good help these days.

She waded through the shin-high snow to one of the many back doors of the mansion and there she repeated the ritual of ring-wait-ring-ring-wait-pound-pound. Still no one answered. She stood a moment and strained her ears for any sounds inside, but everything was quiet. There were no lights on this side of the mansion.

Suddenly it occurred to her that whoever planted the bomb in her car last night could very well have done it here, while she was in the house. So far the police had told her nothing about the design and manufacture of the bomb, but she figured it must have been detonated by a timer. Ordinary pipe bombs were detonated by the ignition, but she'd started her car without incident, and it was twenty minutes later that it blew. And it was only her flat tire that kept her from blowing with it. Whoever planted the bomb must have timed it to detonate on her return to the city. And the only people who could have estimated what time that return trip would take place were the people watching her movements here at Hightower Hill.

It couldn't have been Julia—she was dead to the world—and Marilyn and the gardener seemed very much to be otherwise occupied upstairs. But what about Morgan and his wife, Sissy? She'd seen no sign of them last night. They could have been lurking somewhere in these shadows. They could be lurking there now. . . .

No. Devin gave a firm shake of her head to stop the trail of those thoughts. She'd spent too many years letting fear dictate her life. It was fear of rejection that made her a wallflower all through her teens; it was fear of loneliness that made her marry Milton, the first man who asked her; and it was fear of the dental instruments he used to bring to their bed that made her divorce him soon thereafter—although come to think of it, that particular fear was probably a healthy one. Nonetheless, she wasn't going to let fear control her tonight.

She rang the bell one more time, and when there was still no answer, she reached for the knob and was starting to turn it when a heavy hand squeezed down on her shoulder.

"Oh!" She gasped and spun around in her sodden shoes.

"Oh!" a man's voice exclaimed as he dropped his hand and backed away from her. "Sorry. I didn't know it was you."

She squinted into the shadows and saw that it was only Georges, the landscaping Lothario. "I have an appointment to see Mrs. Hightower," she announced, with more authority than she felt.

"Oh? Funny. You just missed her."

"What?"

"She just drove off in the Bentley, five, maybe ten minutes ago. You wanna come in and wait?" He stepped closer and waggled his eyebrows suggestively. "Maybe have a drink by the fire?"

She shook her head and backed away. "Where did she go?"

"Beats me," he said, then grinned as if he liked the sound of that.

"Okay, thanks." Devin flung the words over her shoulder as she hurried back to the entrance court and jumped into her Taurus.

Julia had left only five or ten minutes ago, there was only one major highway nearby, and the odds were good that she was heading for the city. How hard could it be to find a Bentley heading west on the Long Island Expressway?

*   *   *

NOT HARD, AS it turned out, particularly when that Bentley was traveling at forty miles an hour with the right turn signal flashing. *Warning!* it blinked in semaphore. *Senior Citizen Driving Here.*

Devin pulled up alongside and took a look in the Bentley. It was Julia, all right, and she seemed to be singing at the top of her lungs. Devin waved at her, then tooted the horn, but Julia drove on, merrily oblivious to everything.

Maybe it was better this way, Devin thought. Instead of pulling Julia over, which wasn't working anyway, she'd follow her. Her destination might reveal more than she would ever reveal herself.

Devin dropped back and cut in behind the Bentley and followed it like it was a white Bronco on the Santa Monica Freeway, the only difference being that Julia didn't have a clue she was being followed. Also that there were no helicopters or news cameras tracking her progress. But Devin wondered if her motivation might be the same. Could it be a guilty conscience that was driving Julia's flight? Oh, God, she thought with a sudden sinking in her stomach. Could Julia be suicidal?

She pulled up tighter to the Bentley's bumper and followed at a closer distance as Julia drove on toward the city. She left the Long Island Expressway for the Brooklyn-Queens, then crossed over the Brooklyn Bridge into Lower Manhattan. Was she headed for Wall Street? Devin wondered—but then the Bentley turned left, then left again, and continued south along the East River seaport. Julia seemed to be driving purposefully, although as she passed under a streetlight, Devin could see that she was still singing.

The right blinker switched off for the first time in

thirty minutes, then the left one came on, and slowly the Bentley turned down a narrow street. At the end of it stood a ten-foot-high chain-link fence broken only by a drive-through security gate. The bar of the gate swung high as Julia approached it, and she drove through and made another turn around the corner of a building.

Devin stomped on the gas, but the bar descended before she could follow. She lowered her window and studied the security box, but there was no indication of what was required to open the gate. She backed up and parked in an empty space along the fence, then got out and ducked under the bar and ran after the Bentley.

As she rounded the corner of the building, she realized where she was, and an alarm went off in her brain. This was the Commodore Marina, a place where Wall Street tycoons could conveniently berth their yachts so that when they were in the mood for some ocean air, all they had to do was put on their skipper's caps and order their drivers to take them to the Commodore. Arthur Hightower kept his yacht here, she remembered. It was called the *Silver Girl VI*, the latest descendant of the first *Silver Girl*, which he acquired after cornering the silver market with the Hunt brothers back in the eighties.

Devin spotted the Bentley, and it was heading toward her. She shrank back into the shadows of the clubhouse as it passed. But the driver wasn't Julia. It was a young man in a sailor's cap.

Frantically Devin scanned the marina in search of Julia, and at last she saw her climbing aboard a long gleaming yacht while its captain and crew stood at attention on deck.

"No, wait! Stop!" Devin shouted and sprinted for the yacht. But its engines were already purring; it was slipping out of its berth and moving into the harbor.

"Julia! Don't do this! Come back!" Devin screamed.

But Julia couldn't hear her. She was standing on the forecastle with her head thrown back, her arms flung wide, her mink coat whipping in the wind, and she was singing so loudly that Devin could hear the words where she stood. *"Sail on, Silver Girl, sail on by. . . ."*

"Nooo!" Devin wailed. "Don't do this to me!" She stamped her foot so hard she broke the heel off her shoe, then just to spite herself she stamped the other foot until that heel broke, too. She stood there, three inches shorter, and cursed like a sailor as the yacht glided out to sea and into the black depths of the night.

"Excuse me?" a soft voice spoke behind her. "Aren't you Devin McGee?"

She started to spin on her heels until she remembered she didn't have any. Slowly she turned around. Behind her stood a nice-looking man of about thirty with curly dark hair and big dark eyes. "Devin Gail McGee, to be precise. Who are you?"

"My name's Patrick Roswell."

Her eyes opened wide. "From the *Gazette*?"

"You've heard of me?" he said, amazed.

"Just today. I think we may have a mutual enemy."

"Huh?"

"Six-foot-six, likes to play dress-up?"

"Oh, God," he said, gulping. "He came after you, too?" His eyes darted to her feet.

"Yes," she said, cringing. Her sodden, broken shoes were such a disgrace that this man apparently couldn't keep his eyes off them. She tried to hide one behind the other as she spoke. "He came to my office today and said that you and I should talk."

"Did he tell you how long you had? Because I found out he lied about the thirty-six hours."

"What?" she said, confused.

"He didn't—? I mean—did he hurt you?"

"Well, no. Not really."

"Oh. Good."

Was that relief or resentment in his voice? "Anyway," Devin continued, "I called you today and left a message on your office voice mail. You didn't get it?"

He shook his head glumly. "It's disconnected. I—I got fired today."

"Oh." Devin stared out into the harbor. "What do you know? I think I just got fired, too."

He followed her gaze. "Was that Julia Hightower?"

Devin nodded bitterly.

"Wow," he breathed. "What happens to the murder trial now?"

"If she's not in court tomorrow morning, Judge Hardy will revoke her bail and issue a bench warrant for her arrest. Then he'll probably declare a mistrial and dismiss the panel. Damn it!" she cried. "Why'd she have to pull this stunt now? The message our friend Stretch seemed to be giving me is that she's innocent. But after tonight, everyone will assume she's guilty. I'll never be able to get an untainted jury after this. Even if she comes back."

"But you know," Patrick said hesitantly, "maybe this is a good thing."

"What are you talking about?"

"Stretch gave me the same message. That Julia didn't do it. Devin, there's more to this than meets the eye."

She turned. "That's another thing Stretch said to me."

"Until you—we—figure out what's going on here, maybe it's better to call a time-out in the murder trial."

"When it's out of your control," Devin murmured, "get it out of the courtroom."

"Exactly."

She reflected a moment. Perhaps Julia's *hiatus*—a better word than *flight*—was actually a golden opportunity for Devin to do some digging and try to get to the bottom of all this.

"Wait a minute," she said, her head snapping up. "What are you doing here?"

"Tailing a suspect," Patrick said. He pointed to a smaller yacht at the other end of the marina. "She's in there right now."

Devin's eyes moved between Patrick and the yacht. "Fill me in?" she asked, intrigued.

"Sure. Could we sit someplace—?"

Briefly she considered, then made up her mind and pointed to her car.

PATRICK'S PAIN EVAPORATED in the heat of his excitement as he sat in the front seat of the Taurus and related all he knew about the mysterious woman named Cordelia. But it was the woman named Devin who was making his heart flutter. He couldn't remember ever sitting so close to a woman so lovely. And she was smart, too. He could see the wheels spinning in the irises of her eyes as he told her all about Robert Rutledge and Henry Cloutier and Joe Kellogg.

"So she dropped Henry off at seven," he wound up his tale, "—and broke up with him, too, I'm pretty sure—and drove straight here. She went aboard that boat, the *Starry Night*, a couple of lights went on inside, and I've been waiting here ever since."

Devin nodded musingly. "It must have something to do with Hightower Oil. Remember how Arthur deflected that takeover bid a few years back? What if this Rutledge guy decided to take a run at him? And Arthur just wouldn't budge?"

"I was thinking the same thing," Patrick said. "But is Cordelia working *for* him or *against* him?"

"Look!" Devin's eyes were riveted on the *Starry Night*. "Is that Cordelia?"

A woman stood backlit at one of the windows, still and watchful.

"Yes," Patrick whispered.

"She looks like she's waiting for somebody."

"Maybe we better wait, too."

Devin nodded. After a moment, she reached down and slipped off her shoes and tossed them into the back. A little shiver traveled down Patrick's spine at the intimacy of the gesture.

"I guess—" He stopped and cleared his throat. "I guess you found out that I wasn't really a reporter at the *Gazette*?"

She shrugged. "So? I'm my own secretary and paralegal. There's nothing wrong with wearing multiple hats."

He gazed at her in silence while a symphony played in his head.

Suddenly a grinding of gears sounded behind them; then a wash of headlights poured over the trunk of the Taurus and started to rise up into the rear window.

"Duck!" Devin whispered.

They both dived center and sideways, but Devin dived faster, so Patrick ended up with his chin resting on her back, while her head was rather firmly resting in his lap.

"Umm," Patrick said after a frozen moment. "You think we could switch places here?"

"What? Why?" she whispered, then a second later, "Oh."

He blushed, and she gave him a pat on the knee that was meant, he imagined, to reassure him, though it had a decidedly different effect.

The engine gears ground again, and as the headlights passed up and over the car, Patrick sat up and so did Devin. He shifted uncomfortably to the far side of the seat.

"McGinty's Meats," she said, reading the name on the side of the truck. "Delivering at this hour?"

He jerked forward. "McGinty's!" he exclaimed. "That's where Stretch told me I'd find Joe Kellogg's body."

They watched in horror as two men emerged from the back of the truck, each one grasping a handle of a large freezer chest, which they heaved aboard the *Starry Night*.

"Oh, God," he gasped. "Could that be it?"

"They couldn't fit him into that chest. Could they?"

"Believe me, they could," Patrick said.

Cordelia came out on deck wearing something long and flowing and white. She looked like Ophelia, or maybe Lady Macbeth. One of the truckers handed her a clipboard, and she scanned it, then signed it and handed it back.

"But I don't know," Patrick said. "Seems funny to sign for a corpse."

"Duck," Devin cried again as the truck headed back out the gate.

This time Patrick was ready. He dived first and ended up with his head in Devin's lap.

"Know what I could go for right now?" Devin whispered as they lay motionless across the seats.

"What?" Patrick tried to find the correct way to turn his head. He was no longer sure that this was a better position for him.

"A cheeseburger." The truck passed by, and she sat up straight again.

"You like cheeseburgers?" he said, sitting up.

"Mmm." She closed her eyes dreamily. "Big juicy ones, with the cheese all melted and blistering over it."

Patrick nodded appreciatively.

"And the bun lightly toasted," she went on. "The lettuce and tomato cold and crisp."

He licked his lips.

"With fries on the side, hot and salty."

"Oh, God," he moaned out loud.

A second flash of headlights penetrated the car, and he grabbed Devin and kissed her long and hard.

"Wow," she said, stunned, as they broke apart. "That was fast thinking. I didn't even hear that car coming." She turned to watch as a red sports car slowed for the security gate and then drove through as the bar lifted.

"Know what else I was thinking?" Patrick said, breathing hard. "The Sweeney Hotel seems to be the intersection of a lot of different paths. I think we should go there and check in—I mean, check it out."

"Good idea," she said. "Especially since I'm a little nervous about going to my apartment tonight. Let's get a room at the Sweeney and see what we can find out."

A room? Patrick thought, his heart boomeranging inside his chest. "Great," he gulped.

"Wait a minute," she said sharply.

Damn, he thought.

"That car's headed for the *Starry Night*," she said. "And look—Cordelia's coming out to meet it."

Patrick leaned forward to watch. Cordelia's face was turned down; she seemed to be speaking to someone below her on deck. Then she stooped and lifted a small child into her arms. It was a chubby little toddler, a bouncing baby boy, and she held him close as a man jumped out of the sports car and climbed aboard. Cordelia's face glowed in the starlight as he approached. He took the little boy from her and swung him in the air, then cradled him in the crook of his arm as he leaned in to kiss Cordelia.

"Who is he?" Devin breathed, as all three of the figures on board merged into one.

"Turn around," Patrick urged him in a whisper. "Come on, buddy. Turn around and show your face."

Without turning, the man wrapped his arm around Cordelia's shoulders, and the threesome moved toward the cabin.

"Who are you?" Devin cried.

The man paused on the threshold to look out over the seaport, and for a fraction of a second the starlight shone down on him, just long enough to illuminate the face of Morgan Hightower before he took his mistress and child inside.

CHAPTER

8

"WE NEED TO get on board that boat!" said Devin. Patrick pouted, choked back a protest that he knew would come out as a whine. Boat? What happened to the Sweeney Hotel idea? What happened to the notion of clean sheets and a warm lithe body that might to some degree pay him back for all the humiliations that he'd suffered, and take his mind off the phantom pain he still felt in his absent toe? Then again, he understood that the lissome attorney was absolutely right. Here was an opportunity too crucial to pass up: the mysterious Cordelia linked to the son of Arthur Hightower with, presumably, the elusive carved-up body of Joe Kellogg thrown in for good measure.

Reluctantly, he said, "Okay, okay. But how will we—"

"Wait a second," Devin interrupted. "I can't go. There's no way I can go."

Hope sprang once again into Patrick's heart and other organs. Maybe it would be back to the Sweeney after all.

"Morgan Hightower knows my face," she said. She reflected briefly and with genuine surprise on the unsought fame this case had brought her. "*Everybody* knows my face! You better go alone."

"Excuse me?" Patrick said. He stared miserably across the frozen parking lot, filthy snow piled up at its perimeter. He was hungry. His foot and his prostate were throbbing. It was February. What kind of fool went yachting in February? There could be icebergs out there, for Pete's sake.

Thinking aloud, Devin McGee repeated, "Yes, you better go alone. Because you're, you know . . ."

Because I'm *what*? thought Patrick, with a mix of pique and self-mockery. Because I'm a nobody? Is that what she's thinking? Because no one would recognize a pathetic wuss who's never accomplished anything and who just got fired from his idiotic job? Is that what she's saying about me? In a heartbeat he'd worked himself into a lather of secret indignation. They'd kissed. They'd breathed deeply of each other's laps and come up talking cheeseburgers. After intimacy like that, she was calling him a nobody?

Then he remembered that she'd left her sentence uncompleted. She hadn't called him anything. *He'd* been calling him a nobody.

"Because you're . . . you know . . . a reporter," Devin said.

Patrick blinked at that. Then he smiled and for a brief moment he felt very brave. Yes! He was a reporter! He had no one to report *to*, but that was secondary. The main thing was that he had a story and the will to bulldog it, to see it through. These were fine and manly things and gave him certain privileges. With a new assurance he reached for Devin McGee and kissed her once again. His urgency and her bewilderment caused him to somewhat miss her lips. He sucked her cheek and felt her hair against his neck. Then, feeling as though he were going off to war, he threw open the car door and exited theatrically. His four-toed foot buckled underneath him and made the performance seem a trifle less heroic.

Once outside in the frigid night, his courage soon eroded. He felt a craven impulse to dive back into the Taurus before Devin drove away and all was lost. Instead, he forced himself forward, forming a strategy as he went. He was in a bastion of privilege, he reminded himself. At places like the Commodore Marina, any sign of insecurity would evoke a torrent of suspicion and contempt. The only thing to do was to stand tall and stride onto the grounds like he owned the place. In spite of his cheap clothes. In spite of his ignorance of all things yachty. In spite of everything.

On tingling feet he walked across the frozen parking lot. His breath steamed; the insides of his nostrils stung. But he must have looked at least passingly imposing, because the valet parking guys saluted as he limped by. Bucked up by their gratifying subservience, he continued toward the wharf where the zillion-dollar boats were tied. *Uptick. Acquisition. Dream Chaser.* Most of the boats were dark and battened down, their owners having the sense not to use them in the dead of winter. Only the fleet of the crazy Hightowers saw service now. Passing the vacant berth where *Silver Girl VI* had been, Patrick thought he caught a whiff of gin. But no, that was impossible; it was only his fevered imagination. . . .

He forced his feet to keep moving toward the *Starry Night.* But with every step his jauntiness waned. His posture slumped, and he looked ever less like a visiting admiral and ever more like what he was—an intruder, an uninvited guest, a parvenu. By the time he reached the yacht where Morgan Hightower and Cordelia Baxter were trysting with their little bastard, he was positively skulking, seeking streetlamp shadows, his breath as taut and labored as that of a burglar.

For a moment he just stood there. He saw nothing, heard nothing. The boat, a cabin cruiser, was maybe seventy feet long. Its high sides blocked his view of the interior; the smoked glass of its companionway panels muffled all sound. He looked back across his shoulder, then dared to put a foot up on the transom. From that height, he was tantalized by a hint of soft yellow light from the cabin. He took another step, then one more, and to his own surprise found himself standing in the cockpit, near the wheel.

Dodging into shadow, he studied the scene in the cabin below. It struck him as deflatingly benign, bourgeois. The little bastard was playing with Legos. Morgan and Cordelia were sitting side by side on a leather settee, sipping cocktails like Ozzie and Harriet drank milk. A burly fellow who seemed to be captain, crew, and steward was setting out a plate of canapés. . . . All very cozy. Not exactly the stuff of Pulitzer prizes.

Patrick thought of sneaking out the way he'd come, taking one more shot at luring Devin to the Sweeney. But just then Morgan Hightower gestured toward his hired skipper. The skipper shrugged, then slipped into a peacoat and headed for the companionway. Patrick didn't think, just reacted. There were molded benches in the cruiser's cockpit. The benches were latched; their seats were the lids of storage compartments. Patrick popped one open and dived in. As if he were closing his own coffin, he pulled the cover down just as the captain emerged on deck.

After a moment, the engines started.

Amid the drone and vibration of the diesels, Patrick tried to get comfortable. This proved impossible. He was nestled amid coils of rope and fenders plump as mortadellas. It was freezing cold. It was pitch-dark—except for a louver that vented into the main cabin. Scuttling toward that vent, Patrick found that he could see between the slits; sound came to him above the engine's groan. He hunkered down as lines were released and the *Starry Night* slipped into the icy, fetid waters of the East River.

He watched as Morgan and Cordelia finished up their drinks. Then, rattling the last of his ice, Morgan said, "Hungry?"

Cordelia shrugged. Like many women who trafficked in their beauty, she was loath to admit that her body actually required food.

"Come on," her lover coaxed. He nodded toward the locker from McGinty's, and went on with a leer. "We've got some really special meat."

No! thought Patrick, his eyeballs nearly popping through the vent's narrow slits. Was it possible? The folklore certainly had it that the rich were bloodsuckers . . . but cannibals?

"Perfect rump steaks," said Morgan Hightower.

Oh, my God! thought Patrick. In spite of himself, he pictured Joe Kellogg's backside, perched upon its barstool. Unbidden, the thought came to him that it would probably be very tender, given all the time that lawyers spent sitting on their asses. Unbidden, too, came the old Jeffrey Dahmer line: *So many men, so little freezer space . . .*

"And a nice fresh hot dog for Junior," Morgan said. He turned a goofy face toward his bastard. "Yummy yummy!"

Patrick gagged, whether at the image or the baby talk he could not be sure.

The Hightower heir rose from the settee and went to the meat locker. He opened it. The lid blocked Patrick's view of the contents. He strained to see, expecting . . . what? A bleeding hunk of Kellogg's *tuchas*? Would he even recognize, without context, a severed buttock? Would it look more like a meat loaf or a blancmange? No matter—as Morgan turned away, the would-be reporter could clearly see what he held in his hand. It was . . . beef. Or at least it looked like beef. And the hot dog, to paraphrase Freud, seemed to be only a hot dog.

Patrick sighed. But relief was not unmixed with disappointment. They were not going to eat Joe Kellogg. Then why was he here? He was cramped, trapped—and why? To watch a family have dinner?

Time went very slowly now. The out-of-wedlock family cooked and ate. Shivering and famished amid the ropes and bumpers, Patrick saw no romance in yachting. Finally dinner was finished, dishes were cleared. Then something happened that riveted the stowaway's attention once again.

Morgan Hightower poked his head up toward the companionway and shouted for the captain to come down and help him for a minute. The engines revved down to idle speed. After a moment, Hightower and the skipper could be seen wrestling the meat locker toward the steps between the cabin and the cockpit.

Patrick was confused. Dinner had been eaten. The menu was *boeuf*. Was it conceivable that Kellogg's remains had been in there *with* the *boeuf*? What kind of cockamamie meat order was that? One dead body, two rump steaks, and a hot dog . . .

His eyeballs squeezed against the vent, he watched them climb the stairs. But then they moved into the cockpit and beyond his field of vision. This was unbearable—to have come this far, endured this much, and then to miss the main event. Patrick struggled onto his side. With frozen fingers he punched the latch that held down the compartment cover. He opened it a crack and beheld a weird tableau: a swath of New York skyline; some distance away, a single boat plying the otherwise empty river; and two men swinging a meat locker, working up momentum to pitch it over the side.

Morgan Hightower said, "One . . ."

The burly skipper said, "Two . . ."

They both said, "Three!" And heaved the McGinty's box skyward. It cleared the yacht's railing, but then it started to somersault, and as it somersaulted its lid popped open. The meat box paused an improbable moment at the apex of its flight, and then a head rolled out of it. The head had a dismayed expression on its face. There was still some neck attached to the bottom of it, and a short section of wind-pipe or esophagus stuck out like an electrical connector or a sprinkler attachment.

Patrick retched. Loudly. So loudly that his retching could be heard above the splash of body parts and meat locker.

The other two men turned in his direction. The hapless Patrick slammed shut his compartment. Too late. The burly captain opened it again, reached down, and lifted him out by his coat. He tried to bring him to his feet, but Patrick's ravaged and frozen toes wouldn't let him stand.

"Who the hell are you?" demanded Morgan Hightower.

Patrick couldn't speak. The severed head still swam before his eyes. He mumbled, "Ah, erg, um . . ."

The Hightower heir, as though he'd just now noticed, said, "Christ, it's cold out here."

Patrick said, "Hnnn, brrr, duhhhh . . ."

The captain looked at his boss. In his eyes was a mute question as to the imbecilic stowaway's fate. Morgan Hightower just nodded.

And Patrick felt himself launched from the skipper's grasp, over the yacht's side, and down, down into the river's filthy frigid water, presumably to join the myriad corpses, whole and sundered, already gathered there like urban sediment, the suicides and rubouts, those who'd swan-dived off the Brooklyn Bridge and those who wore cement shoes. The East River, Patrick thought in the instant before losing consciousness—at least it was a fabled place to die.

"*FOR WHO WOULD* blank *bear?*" said Henry Cloutier.

"Fardels," said Devin McGee.

"I haven't even said how many letters," said the night watchman at Miller Tool and Die.

"Trust me," Devin said. "It's fardels. It's Shakespeare."

Cloutier, with his penchant for brainy women, was impressed. "Fits," he said, his lips moving as he counted out the spaces. "What's a fardel?"

"I have no idea. No one does. Maybe Shakespeare didn't even know. But listen, Henry, I didn't come here to do crossword puzzles."

In fact she'd gone to Miller Tool and Die because it was the only move she could think of that might conceivably be useful. She'd waited in the parking lot of the

Commodore Marina until the *Starry Night* had loosed
its dock lines and motored off, taking Patrick with it.
Watching it go, she'd suddenly felt helpless and empty.
Her client had taken it on the lam. Her one ally—whose
unexpected kisses now tingled in her memory—was
being swept off God knows where. Maybe she could at
least learn more about the versatile Cordelia.

But Henry Cloutier was still thinking about fardels.
"Maybe they're, like, small farts? Silent ones?"

"Maybe," Devin conceded. "But Henry—Patrick told
me you started on this crossword kick to impress
Cordelia. Isn't that true?"

"Yup," he said laconically. They were sitting in his
tiny office. A bank of closed-circuit monitors confirmed
that nobody was breaking in. Of course they weren't.
There was nothing worth stealing at the Tool and Die.
How did you fence a two-ton lathe?

"But I thought Cordelia just broke up with you," the
lawyer pressed.

Henry bit his lip, as if fending off heartbreak. "I'm not
convinced it's final. Besides, now I seem to be addicted to
the stupid things. Oh, here's one: *If a* blank *be washed
to sea* . . ."

"Clod."

"Now, miss," said Henry. "That isn't nice. I never said
I was the smartest. I'm just a simple working man trying
to better myself."

"If a *clod* be washed to sea," said Devin. "John Donne."

"Hey, you're a whiz at this. Got a boyfriend?"

"Yes," she lied. "I do. But about Cordelia—how did
you two meet?"

Henry's eyes took on a faraway look. "I guess you
could say it was fate."

"I guess you could say everything is fate," said Devin. "That's why they call it fate. Could you be a little more specific?"

The watchman sighed. "Gee, I don't know. It's a little bit embarrassing. Truth is, it was a rebound kind of thing."

"Rebound?"

Henry squirmed, sought refuge in his puzzle. "Wait," he said, "here's a long one. *Journalistic poultry dish?*"

"Pullet surprise," said Devin. "But Henry—rebound from *what?*"

He put his pencil down and exhaled slowly. "Okay. Okay. Used to be," he said, "that when I finished my shift here, I'd go up to the Sweeney for a nightcap. I met Cordelia in the bar up there, late on a night when she'd been dumped by someone else. She was a mess. Half-drunk. Teary. That's why it's embarrassing. I don't kid myself. She would never have been interested in me, except I found her at a very vulnerable moment."

"Who dumped her, Henry? Who'd she been with?"

"I don't know. She didn't say a name. I didn't ask."

"And you never talked about it after?"

"Hey," he said, "the past is past."

Devin briefly pondered, thinking about Cordelia with deep disapproval and maybe just a touch of envy. She was Morgan's mistress *plus* she had another guy *plus* she took up with the watchman the same night she got dumped? "Henry," she said, "do you remember what night this was?"

"Oh, yes," he said, "I remember very well. November the fourth."

"The fourth!" said Devin. "Isn't that the night you saw Arthur Hightower . . . ?"

"It is," said Henry. "I told Patrick that I took Cordelia

to the Sweeney. That was a little fib, to save face for both of us. But the truth is she started the evening with some-one else, and ended it with me."

"But you don't know who?"

Infuriatingly, the little watchman shrugged and went back to his puzzle. The lawyer tried a different tack.

"Has anyone ever said you look just like Robert Rutledge?"

"Who?"

With only limited success Devin fought off exaspera-tion. "Don't you read the papers?"

"Sure I do. The sports page. And the crossword."

"But not the business section?"

"What's that got to do with me?" said Henry.

Her frustration clear now, Devin exhaled loudly as she rose to go.

"Before you go, miss—one more clue? *A woman, to some*. Four letters. The last three are *u-n-t*."

Devin thought for just a moment. "Aunt," she said.

"Ah, nuts," said the watchman. "Got an eraser?"

IN WATER AS cold as the East River in February, a human being, even if he doesn't drown, will be dead of hypo-thermia in around seven minutes. But that leaves out the sludge factor. Ever notice how English Channel swim-mers smear themselves with Vaseline? This is not just product placement or a sensual thing. The petroleum locks in body heat like an external layer of artificial fat.

So it was when Patrick Roswell went flailing and groaning through the surface. A disgusting goo—the spillage from archaic tugboats and abattoirs in Queens and asphalt plants up in the Bronx—coated him from head to toe, sealed him in a quasi-amniotic slime. Say what you want about pollution—it saved Patrick's life, bought him just enough time so that when the boat he'd seen from the deck of *Starry Night* reached him, he was still alive—just barely. He'd stopped his kicking and his screaming. He was utterly inert and had all but given up on breathing.

A cool, blue-tinged euphoria had mercifully descended on him. Death, he somehow understood, could be sweeter than life. When the grappling hook seized him by the armpit, and he felt himself being yanked and lugged, water streaming off him as if he were a breaching porpoise, he imagined he was being *shlepped* to Heaven.

He wasn't. He was being dragged into the cockpit of a boat, where several excited men were trying to determine whether he was still alive, and what the hell they should do with him. A hand felt for his jugular. Another pressed on his belly; he vaguely felt himself vomiting water. In Patrick's comalike state, he couldn't speak, couldn't get his eyes to open—yet he could hear quite clearly every word that was said.

"The thing to do," a baritone announced, "is strip him naked and get in bed with him."

"You do it, Joe," said another man. "I hear you like that kind of thing."

"Don't knock it if you haven't tried it."

"Har, har har!"

Vaguely, Patrick thought, I'm dying here, and they're making gay jokes. . . .

Then he heard a woman say, "What's all the commotion?"

Everyone tried to explain at once.

The woman said, "Oh, my God! Bring him down, bring him down."

Patrick felt himself being carried. Felt himself being stripped and laid into a bed. He sensed an enveloping warmth, gradually understood that someone was lying next to him, that arms were wrapped around him and that a tummy was pressed against his own. He had no idea how long they lay like that. But over time he grew warm enough to shiver. Then his teeth began to chatter, and a little after that he started to moan. Something like consciousness began to dawn again. His eyes still closed, he sobbed.

The woman next to him stroked his head and said, "It's all right now. It's all right."

Patrick was slightly conscious now. Conscious enough to realize that he'd nearly died. Conscious enough to know that he was naked and in bed with a naked woman. For some reason he thought about the tragedy and triumph of the salmon. The chilly, desperate swim upstream to spawn. The sex that meant both death and final victory. He'd done his swim, by God. He'd earned some ecstasy. Tentatively, he made a small thrust with his hips. His bedmate did not recoil, and he was heartened. Still, there was the matter of confidence. Or the lack thereof. Growing less certain even as he grew more aroused, Patrick thought, *Maybe if she thinks I'm in a coma, she'll let me . . .*

He kept his eyes closed. He moaned as he rolled on top of her. The ruse was unnecessary. Julia Hightower, feeling more alive than she had felt in ages, would have gratefully accepted the advances of this needy stranger no matter what.

CHAPTER
9

FOR THE FIRST time in recent memory, Julia Hightower did not feel the need for a drink. Even if she'd wanted one, she wouldn't have had the strength to call for it.

Julia rolled onto her side and studied the young man the captain of the *Silver Lady VI* had dragged from the icy clutches of the East River. Her aquatic Casanova had passed out after their first savage coupling and she had not learned his name. When he awoke again, Julia lost interest in everything but his questing hands, searching tongue, and thrusting lance.

Patrick moaned and opened his eyes slowly. Julia ran a finger along his chest.

"You saved me," he said.

"I'd say you've paid me back in full," Julia replied. And, in truth, Patrick's enthusiastic lovemaking had thawed out Julia Hightower as much as she had thawed him out.

"Where am I?"

"Safe and sound aboard my yacht."

Patrick sat up. "It feels like your yacht is moving."

"It is, my love. It's speeding us to a warm and indolent land where we can spend our days basking in the hot sun and our nights . . . Well, I'll let you figure that out."

The curtains were drawn in the stateroom and the lights were off. While he was in the throes of passion, Patrick had not gotten a good look at the tigress whose bed he shared. Now that his eyes were beginning to adjust to the dark, his rescuer was starting to look familiar.

"Do I know you?" he asked.

"Why do you want to know?" Julia asked nervously.

Patrick's brow furrowed as he put the woman's features together with a name the way he put answers to clues when he did the daily crossword.

"Julia Hightower!"

"And, if I were?" Julia answered tremulously, terrified that her merman would flee their aquarium of love once he discovered that he'd engaged in sexual congress with a notorious alleged murderess.

Patrick took Julia's hands in his. "Then I might be able to help you."

Julia was puzzled. "Help me how?"

"To clear your name."

"How can you do that?"

"I've been investigating your husband's murder and I've uncovered some very disturbing facts."

"Why would you be investigating Arthur's death? Are you a detective?"

"No, I'm a reporter."

Julia's mouth opened in terror.

"Oh, no, you don't have to worry. I'm not a real reporter, yet. Although I hope to be, once I break this story. Actually, I sold ads for the *Gazette*, before they fired me. I guess it would be more accurate to say that I'm an aspiring reporter. In any event, I believe I've uncovered a conspiracy to frame you for Arthur Hightower's murder."

"A conspiracy? But who . . . ?"

"I'm not certain, but you have to be very careful. The people involved in this will stop at nothing. They've chopped off my toe. . . ."

"Your toe!" Julia echoed in horror.

Patrick nodded. "And they tried to drown me when I saw them disposing of Joe Kellogg's severed head."

"Joe! Headless!"

Patrick squeezed Julia's trembling hands. "Don't worry," he assured her. "We'll get to the bottom of this."

"What do you mean 'we'?"

"Working together, we can solve this mystery, prove your innocence, and win me a Pulitzer prize."

"The only thing I'm going to work on is my tan," Julia said sadly. "I'm going to Panga Nue, where it's always summer and the islanders don't extradite."

She ran her hand through Patrick's hair and kissed him passionately.

"Forget about this foolishness and come away with me."

"You can't run."

"What do I have to go back to? A cold and drafty house, two ungrateful children, and a future on death row?"

"Everyone will think you're guilty if you run. They'll stop looking for the real killer. You've got to turn the yacht around before the police find out you tried to flee."

"Not on your life."

Patrick took Julia in his arms and felt her heart beat strongly against his chest.

"We just met, Julia. I don't want to lose you."

And this was true. Kissing Devin McGee had been pretty neat, but Patrick had never lived through a night of love like the one he had experienced with Julia Hightower. Granted, his experience was limited, and the circumstances of this tryst were a tad unusual, but Julia's sexual acrobatics had made his hair stand on end and his toes curl—all nine of them.

"What about the difference in our ages, my love?"

"Love knows no boundaries, my sweet."

"Oh . . ." Julia paused. "I don't even know your name."

"It's Patrick. Patrick Roswell."

"Oh, Patrick," Julia moaned.

Patrick felt Julia's breasts swell and he heard her sigh.

"You're not alone anymore, Julia. You have me by your side. And, together, we'll lick this thing."

"I'm frightened," Julia said as her hand snaked between them. "Hold me tight."

Patrick's eyes glazed over and his breath came in short gasps.

"Tell me once more about this licking thing," Julia whispered.

SNOW WAS FALLING hard when Devin drove away from Miller Tool and Die, and she had to concentrate on the road. That's why she did not notice the car that followed her as soon as she pulled away from the curb. When Devin wasn't concentrating on the road, she was trying to figure out her next move. There was one thing she knew that she had to do: she had to stop court from reconvening. It looked as if Julia was on the lam. If she did not show up, Judge Hardy would revoke her bail and she would become a fugitive. Any jury would look at flight as a sign of guilt and Julia could kiss her chances of an acquittal good-bye. But how could she stop the trial? It suddenly occurred to her that she knew someone who might be persuaded to help her. There was a big risk involved, but she decided to take it.

Devin drove to Trent Ballard's apartment house in the hope that Trent would agree to set over the case until she could contact Julia and try to talk her into coming back. If that failed, Devin was prepared to go to Judge Hardy and ask for a mistrial. She would inform the judge about her tryst with Trent at the convention and claim that there was a conflict of interest if Trent remained on the case. She would tell the judge that Trent's last-minute appointment had surprised her and it had taken her a while to work out the ethical implications. There was a danger that Trent would want his quickie with Devin becoming general knowledge around the courthouse. Bragging about his hot-tub adventure would help Trent heighten his reputation as a lady-killer. But Devin hoped that Trent would be enough of a gentleman to agree to the set over in chambers, so the press would not learn the reason for it.

Devin found a parking spot across from Trent's apartment. Devin ran through the snow and was covered with flakes by the time she reached the shelter of the lobby. Trent's apartment was on the top floor. Devin took the elevator up. She was surprised to find the door to Trent's apartment open. The assistant D.A. was sitting on the couch staring at something. Devin entered the apartment.

"Trent?"

He looked up and Devin could see that the D.A. was scared.

"They killed him."

Devin followed his gaze and her mouth opened in horror. There was a lighting fixture in the center of Trent's living room and Buck, his pet rabbit, was swinging back and forth from it. Pinned to Buck's chest was a note: YOU'VE BEEN WARNED.

When they were in the hot tub, Trent had told Devin about Buck. His affection for the fluffy animal had seduced her and, in the heat of passion, he'd actually called her his "wittle wabbit."

Devin closed and locked the hall door, then sat beside Trent on the sofa. She put an arm around his shoulders and knew that his sorrow was real when he made no attempt to grope her.

"Who did this?" Devin asked.

"I've been a fool, Devin," Trent said. "I've gotten in over my head."

"Does this have anything to do with Arthur Hightower's murder?"

Trent nodded. Devin pushed Trent away, held him by his shoulders, and looked him in the eye.

"What have you done?"

Trent made eye contact for a moment. Then his head dropped.

"I can't tell you."

"Why?"

"If it got out, my career would be over and I could be putting you in danger."

"Trent, I came here to talk to you about Julia's case. There are a lot of things that you don't know. I'm certain Julia was framed for Arthur's murder, but I don't know who is behind the frame. If we put what you know together with what I know, we might be able to break this case wide open."

Trent considered what she'd said. Then he sighed.

"The day it was announced that I was taking over the case, Marilyn Hightower approached me while I was walking Buck. I had no idea who she was, but she was gorgeous, sexy, and had nothing but nice things to say about Buck. One thing led to another and we ended up here.

"While we were . . . you know, she wheedled out of me the fact that I was trying the Hightower case. She asked if she could see the evidence. I resisted at first, but she broke me down. I snuck her into my office at two in the morning. When she saw the autopsy photos, Marilyn grew faint, or she pretended to be faint. When I came back with a glass of water, she seemed to be better.

"On the way back to my place, Marilyn revealed that she was Arthur Hightower's daughter. I was stunned. She said that no one needed to know that she had been alone with the evidence and she hinted that she had done something to it. I knew I would be through if I told anyone.

"Last night, Marilyn visited me again. She said that she wanted me to do something when the trial resumed."

"What?"

"I don't know. I told her I didn't want to know what it was and I wouldn't do anything more. She told me to think about it. Then she left. A short time later, someone called and said they had absolute proof that your client killed Arthur Hightower. We arranged to meet, but no one showed up. When I got back here . . ."

Trent could not go on.

"Do you think Marilyn is behind this?"

"Who else could be?"

"I think that there are two groups at work."

Devin told Trent about the cross-dressing assassin who was trying to help Julia and some of the other things she'd learned.

"So you think the people who are trying to keep Morgan and Marilyn from inheriting killed Buck to scare me away from helping Marilyn?"

"I don't know. Marilyn isn't in this alone. I'm certain of that. The people she's working with could have killed Buck to force you to do what Marilyn wants."

Trent was about to say something when he noticed the knob on the hall door turning. He put a finger to his lips and crossed the room quietly. Then he wedged a chair under the doorknob. In the silence, Trent and Devin could hear someone picking the lock. Trent gestured toward his bedroom. As soon as they were inside, Trent locked the bedroom door and opened the window. There was a fire escape outside it. Devin ducked her head and crawled through the window. She was hit immediately by a blast of freezing air that rocked her backward. Trent followed and closed the window just as the front door shattered. He pointed down and Devin began descending the ice-coated iron steps. Her foot slipped and she started to fall. Trent's strong fingers clamped onto her arm and arrested her flight. She took one deep breath then started down again.

Trent was right behind her, urging Devin to move faster. When they were halfway down, the window of

Trent's apartment exploded and slivers of glass mixed with the falling snow. One large shard just missed Devin's cheek because she flung herself against the ladder. Someone shouted, "There they are!" and Devin looked up to see two men in peacoats and ski masks racing down the ladder after them.

Devin sped up her descent and widened the distance between her and her pursuers. The alleyway at the side of Trent's building was only a story away. They would be able to drop into the snow in a moment more and race to her car. Relief spread through her, then instantly turned to fear. The alley dead-ended against a building and someone was blocking the opening to the street.

WHEN THEY WERE sated, Julia and Patrick lay side by side with their hands entwined.

"I can't believe that Arthur was the victim of a conspiracy," Julia said.

"Conspiracies do exist, Julia, and you're enmeshed in one."

"But who . . . ?"

"Your son, Morgan, for one."

"Morgan!" Julia laughed. "He doesn't have the brains or the energy to conspire against someone."

"You may have underestimated Morgan. He's the one who gave the order to throw me overboard from the *Starry Night*."

"But why would he do that?"

"I saw him tossing Joe Kellogg's head into the river."

"Morgan murdered Joe?"

"No. He might have given the order but I'm certain

that a seven-foot-tall maniac in a clown outfit, who likes to torture people, killed Kellogg."

"But why?"

"Have you ever heard of Robert Rutledge?"

Julia frowned. "That name sounds familiar, but . . . no."

"Cordelia, Morgan's mistress, is his personal assistant."

"Morgan has a mistress?"

"And an illegitimate child, I suspect."

"Hmm. Maybe there's more to Morgan than I thought."

"Rutledge is the head of Hammer, Crain and Rutledge, a Wall Street firm that made an unsuccessful attempt to take over Hightower Oil. The attempt failed because Arthur blocked it. With Arthur dead, I think Rutledge is trying again. Kellogg was Hammer Crain's attorney. If you're convicted, Morgan and Marilyn inherit everything, including control of Hightower Oil. I think Kellogg was trying to get Morgan and Marilyn to sell that control to Rutledge. Cordelia, Morgan's mistress, started working for Rutledge. I think Morgan talked Cordelia into being his mole in Hammer Crain."

Something Patrick had said started Julia thinking. "From what you've told me, Morgan and Marilyn have the best motives for killing Arthur and framing me. One thing that links me to Arthur's murder is the pearl necklace that he had in his hand when we found him. But I'm not the only one who had a string of pearls like the one Arthur was clutching: Morgan and Marilyn had identical pearl necklaces."

A determined look took hold of Julia's features. She stood up and called to the captain.

"Turn around. We're heading back to shore."

Patrick smiled. "I knew you wouldn't quit and run."

"I'm convinced that Morgan or Marilyn murdered Arthur," she said. "All we have to do is find out which of them is missing a pearl necklace and we'll have our killer."

SISSY HIGHTOWER LIVED at the Hightower estate, but she kept an apartment in Brooklyn Heights under the name of Jacqueline Dupré. Sissy had told Morgan that she was visiting a girlfriend in the city and would sleep at her apartment. Morgan had not seemed to care. In fact, he'd encouraged her to spend as much time as she wanted, which was okay by Sissy, because she could take him for only so long. Marrying Morgan had been a means to an end, but she'd paid a big price. Thank God, Morgan had almost no sex drive. When they did make love it gave new meaning to the idea of having a quickie.

Keeping in shape was important for a spy. Whenever she had the chance, Sissy practiced Mo Ped, an exotic martial art developed in the jungles of Togo, pumped iron, and ran. Tonight, Sissy was finishing a ten-mile run by crossing the Brooklyn Bridge on the way back to her apartment. She was dressed in black, skintight spandex pants and a black windbreaker, and a rape whistle hung around her neck. Her hood was up, concealing her face. A section of the bridge was in the shadows cast by one of the massive steel supports. Stefan Ghorse stepped into her path.

"Nice togs," he said.

Sissy stopped short. She was always amazed that someone Stefan's size, dressed as bizarrely as he usually dressed, could move so quietly and go unnoticed. Then she remembered that they were in New York, the only city on Earth where a cross-dressing giant looks normal.

"Jesus, Stefan, you scared the shit out of me."

"That was my intention."

He was holding a silenced pistol and it was aimed between her ample breasts.

"I like your outfit," Sissy said sarcastically. The behemoth was dressed in skintight Lycra and a wig, pulled back in a ponytail. He would be a mirror image of Sissy—if Sissy were a professional basketball player.

Stefan pointed toward Sissy's Nike Trainers. "Nice sneakers, gringo. I like your sneakers. Maybe you give me your sneakers?" he said in a bad Mexican accent.

"*The Treasure of the Sierra Madre.*"

"Right, but you only get one point. It was too easy."

"What's the gun for?"

Ghorse smiled sadistically.

"We're going to do something I've always wanted— have a nice chat in a secluded place. I always thought that you could stand a lot of pain. Now I'm going to find out."

If I can take this drivel, I can take anything, Sissy thought, but out loud she said seductively, "I'm not big on torture, but we could go someplace quiet and do something else."

She winked and Stefan shook his head.

"That wasn't very convincing, Sissy. Sorry, I have my orders from the O. If you'd followed yours, instead of interfering with the Organization's plans for Hightower Oil, I wouldn't have to kill you."

"Can't we work something out?" she begged. "I couldn't help it if I fell in love with Morgan. You can't punish me for that."

Stefan laughed. "The only person you've ever been in love with is yourself."

Sissy grabbed hold of the whistle she wore around her neck.

"Go ahead and blow," Stefan snickered, flicking the point of his pistol in either direction. "Who's going to hear you?"

Cars were whizzing by too fast for their drivers to suspect that anything unusual was going on between the two people dressed in jogging gear, and there were no runners or bicyclists anywhere near them.

Sissy pointed the mouth of the whistle at Stefan and pressed the concealed trigger. The .45 caliber slug smashed into Stefan and sent him tumbling backward over the bridge railing.

"*Hasta la vista,*" Sissy yelled to his fast-disappearing form. She started to turn, but stopped when she thought she heard Stefan yelling back in a bad Austrian accent. The phrase he screamed sounded like, "I'll be Bach."

Sissy was puzzled. Why, at the moment of his death, would Stefan want to be a composer of classical music? Perhaps he believed in reincarnation. Sissy shook her head. Everyone faced death differently.

Sissy reloaded her whistle and started back to her apartment. If Stefan had been ordered by the O to torture and kill her, another assassin would be hot on her heels as soon as the Organization learned that Stefan had failed. She'd have to evacuate immediately.

Sissy quickened her pace and started thinking about her next move. She was so preoccupied it never occurred to her that she had never heard the splash she would have heard if Stefan's body had crashed into the river.

*   *   *

JULIA'S DRIVER PARKED her limousine in front of the massive wooden front doors of the Hightower mansion. Julia and Patrick had been preoccupied during the ride from the marina and it took them a moment to realize that something was wrong.

"Why aren't there any lights?" Patrick asked.

Julia was sitting on the side farthest from the house and she had to duck her head to see the ground floor through the tinted windows.

"Gustave," she called to her driver, "please accompany us and bring your gun."

"Very well, madam," answered the broad-shouldered German who served as the Hightower's chauffeur.

Gustave opened Julia's door and Patrick followed her into the driving snowstorm. Gustave preceded the couple up the front steps. He tried the door and it creaked when he pushed it open.

"The door should have been locked," Julia said. "Why didn't Harcourt get the door?"

"I don't know, madam, but I don't like this," Gustave replied. "Perhaps you should stay in the front hall while I see if there is anything wrong."

Gustave flipped a switch next to the front door and the light from a huge chandelier bathed the front hall. Julia gasped. Harcourt, the Hightower butler, was crumpled at the bottom of a staircase that curved upward toward the second floor. Gustave knelt next to him and felt for a pulse.

"He's alive," the chauffeur said. "I suggest you call 911 and ask for an ambulance."

Julia used the phone on the entryway table while Gustave climbed the stairs to the second floor. She was finishing the 911 call when Gustave reappeared. He face was drained of color.

"What is it?" Julia asked.

"I think you'd better come upstairs and look at this," Gustave replied.

CHAPTER
10

Julia felt her heart wrench with a violence that shocked her almost as much as the scene itself. Her only son lay on his back on the hardwood floor in his studio, his limbs hideously askew and his head resting in a spreading pool of blood. Though Julia could see no apparent injury, she knew the truth as soon as she saw him: *Morgan was dead.* The obscenity of his lifeless form contrasted cruelly with the delicacy of the landscapes and portraits propped on easels and leaning against the walls of the studio.

Morgan was dead. Instinct made Julia cry out and drove her to Morgan's side, where she knelt down and grasped his chilly hand with a love she wished she had summoned before, when her son was still alive. Tears filled her eyes as she gazed down at his profile, which revealed the blond, childish curls behind his ears. She flashed oddly on scenes of Morgan as a small boy, a mental photo album of the days before drink drowned her memories, even the happiest ones: *Morgan, learning to pump his legs on the tire swing out back; Morgan, running in short pants to the lake in the summertime; Morgan, playing with the eight-color set of watercolors that became his one and only interest.*

"Morgan," Julia whispered hoarsely, hearing the emotion in her own voice, and the shame. She was ashamed of herself, of her conduct as a mother. She had failed Morgan, failed her family. Her children—her *own children*—couldn't help but fall away. There was no mother to bind them; no core to hold them fast. The Hightowers were a family without a heart, all because of her. Julia's remorse ran deep as a river, and she knew now it would be as eternal. She squeezed Morgan's hand again, willing life into it futilely.

"I am so sorry, Morgan," she whispered, but knew that it didn't make a difference. His hand chilled hers to the bone. His form lay motionless. A vermilion blotch lay at the center of his chest and his blood pooled around him, drying in the cracks of the maple floorboards, soaking the grain of the light wood. Morgan's body was turned slightly away, so the single bullethole over his heart edged discreetly outside Julia's field of vision, and for that small mercy she was grateful. She couldn't bear to focus on the fatal wound or the blood that trailed from it to the floor and reached in a rivulet to an empty canvas stretched over a plywood frame. Yet to be painted, the canvas was now splashed with crimson. Morgan's lifeblood.

Julia looked away as she held tight to her son's hand. She willed herself to comprehend what she was seeing and how it had happened. A small gray gun lay at Morgan's side, just beyond his fingertips, curled in death.

Next to the gun lay a paintbrush with a black handle and
beyond that a canvas, which had been scrawled upon
with black acrylic paint, evidently from the discarded
brush. The letters loomed as large and crude as a home-
made sign, though Julia couldn't bring herself to read it.

Patrick, standing slightly behind Julia, leaned over and
squinted at the canvas. " 'I am my own worst painting,' "
he read aloud. " 'My taste, and my timing, are simply
awful. I fear I have overstayed. Forgive me. Love, M.' "

Julia heard Patrick's voice as if it were coming from
far away. For a minute, the paintings surrounding her
seemed to swirl like spin art at a country fair, trans-
formed into pinwheels blazing with rich blues, reds, and
golds, making her dizzy and sick at heart.

"That's a suicide note," Patrick said softly. "I guess
Morgan killed himself."

Suicide? It wasn't possible. "No," Julia said, almost
reflexively, and Patrick looked at her with sympathy.

"Is it Morgan's handwriting?" he asked, and Julia
forced herself to look at the canvas.

"Yes."

"Is it what he would say, how he speaks? 'I fear I
have—' "

"Yes, but that's beside the point."

"I don't think so. He shot himself in the chest, Julia.
Everything here indicates it. I'm really sorry," Patrick
said, his hand touching her shoulder.

But none of it made sense, not to Julia, who was thinking
like a mother for the first time in her life. She knew her son,
and this wasn't the act of her son. How could she have ever
suspected him of killing Arthur? Morgan wasn't a killer. Or
a suicide. "But what about Harcourt, downstairs? If this
is a suicide, what happened to him?"

"The medics just took him to the hospital."

"Wasn't he shot as well? It seemed like someone broke in to the house and shot Harcourt, then came up and shot Morgan."

"No. Harcourt wasn't shot, Julia." Patrick touched her shoulder tenderly. "You ran upstairs too soon, to see what was the matter with Morgan. There wasn't a mark on Harcourt. It wasn't foul play. The medics think he had a heart attack."

"A heart attack?" Julia frowned.

"Yes. He must have come upstairs—maybe after he heard the gunshot coming from the studio—and the surprise of Morgan's suicide gave him a heart attack."

Julia shook her head. "Then how did he get downstairs?"

"He may have staggered down, trying to reach the telephone to call 911. There's a phone at the end of the stairway on a table. You used it yourself."

"But what about the front door?" Questions about the scenario flooded Julia's brain. "It was left open, as if someone had broken in."

"I didn't see any signs of a break-in, so maybe somebody left it open by accident. Half the time, I leave my keys in my front door, like an idiot. Plus, with the snowstorm, the wind could have blown it ajar if it wasn't fastened properly."

"But still." Julia couldn't stop shaking her head, her tears clearing. She knelt at Morgan's side and couldn't let go of his hand. "Why would Morgan kill himself?"

"If he was mixed up in this conspiracy to set you up, maybe he felt bad about it." Patrick thought about it. "Maybe he changed his mind. Nobody could enjoy framing his mother."

Julia winced inwardly. As bad a mother as she had been, she may have deserved life in prison, but Morgan didn't have the heart to send her there, not even as a decision he would later regret. "No, that's not it."

"Why not?"

"For one thing, then the note doesn't make sense." She pointed to the scrawled canvas, her free hand trembling, and Patrick took it gently and tried to lift her to her feet, a comforting gesture that Julia pressed away in abrupt refusal.

"What's the matter? I'm just trying to help," Patrick said, the pain in his eyes as evident as a child's, touching Julia's heart. Patrick *was* a child in a sense, probably half her age. Patrick was *Morgan's* age. Julia shuddered, realizing that she didn't belong with someone so young. She fumbled to recover her dignity, long hidden in a golden haze of whiskey and denial.

"Patrick," she said firmly, "if you want to help me, stop being my lover. Be my friend."

"What? How?"

Patrick's bewilderment was palpable, and Julia chose her words carefully: "I'm certain this isn't a suicide. This is murder."

"Julia, why?"

"If there's a conspiracy, perhaps Morgan uncovered it and was going to bring it to light. If someone is framing me for murder, maybe he found out who it was. I don't know the particulars, but I'm going to find out." Julia gave Morgan's hand one final squeeze of good-bye, then rose quickly despite her still-weak knees. "Let's go."

"Where?"

"To the hospital. Poor Harcourt was alive when I left him." Julia's tone was urgent, though over Patrick's shoulder she spotted Morgan's half-finished portrait of Sissy resting on an easel. In the portrait her daughter-in-law's strand of pearls stared Julia in the face. *Sissy*. Sissy could have murdered Morgan to get the inheritance, and it would serve her to make it look like a suicide. It had to be Sissy who killed Morgan, her own husband. "I bet Sissy killed Morgan. Harcourt can tell us if I'm right and exactly how Morgan died. And where is Sissy anyway? She's supposed to live here."

"Julia, Harcourt may not be able to tell us anything. The man had a cardiac arrest." Patrick looked dubious. "He was barely breathing when they took him away. They even had to revive him when they got him on the stretcher. He'd be in no shape to identify Sissy or anyone else."

"You don't know that for sure. Let's hurry. There's no time to lose." Julia crossed to the door where Gustave stood and didn't look back at Patrick, the portrait of Sissy, or the slain body of her son. She didn't want to remember Morgan that way, and the only help she could give him now was to find his killer. She owed him at least that much, and it was a debt she intended to pay in full.

"Julia! Wait!" Patrick shouted after her, but Julia was confronting a startled Gustave, the chauffeur.

"Give me your gun," she demanded.

"But, madam, why?"

"I may need it." Julia felt stronger, thinking clearly now, empowered by her venom for Sissy. Julia wasn't sure what she'd do with the gun, but she was certain it would come in handy. "I can't take the gun on the floor, it's evidence left by the killer."

Gustave backed away. "But, ma'am, my gun is fully loaded."

"Splendid. It works better that way."

"But, madam—"

"Give it to me, Gustave!" Julia ordered, her old haughtiness returning, but this time she welcomed it. For Morgan. She opened her palm and Gustave slid his gun from his shoulder holster and reluctantly placed it in her palm. For the first time in her life, Julia thanked a servant.

Then she sprinted for the stairway, her pumps clattering down the marble hallway, with Patrick right behind her.

HER HEART POUNDING with fear and exertion, Devin squinted as she ran, frantic to see who was blocking her and Trent's escape to the street. It was too dark to see a damn thing. "Trent!" she shouted, panicky. "Who is that? What is that?"

"Just keep running! They're gaining on us!" Trent shouted to her, then glanced over his shoulder. The two men in ski masks clambered down the fire escape and were closing the gap between them. Suddenly one raised a gun as he ran. Adrenaline surged through Trent's body. "Go! Go! *Go!*" he called out, and Devin heard the fear in his voice and put on the afterburners in the snow.

Devin and Trent ran stride for stride at the dark figure, tacitly choosing the lesser of two evils. One death, at the hands of the ski-masked men, was certain; and the other was less so. It turned out to be the safe bet.

Devin would have laughed with relief if she weren't so terrified. The figure was a homeless man dancing a little jig on the sidewalk, surrounded by a small crowd and inspired by a tune only he heard. Still, Devin didn't want to run him over, even though he seemed unaware that two lawyers were running full-speed toward him. It was a sight that would have sent any sane person running for cover, but the homeless man was clearly not any sane person. Bedraggled clothes hung on his small form, his wild eyes and other features all but obscured by the dark alley and the dirt on the man's face. In a minute, the lawyers and the homeless would collide, and Trent was thinking the same way as Devin.

"Get out of the way!" Trent called to the man. "They've got a gun! Call the cops!"

"Help us! Help!" Devin shouted, with her last breath. The crowd scattered, sensing danger, but the homeless man kept dancing.

They ran faster. The ski masks were almost upon them, taking aim. But the street was crowded. Would they shoot anyway? Devin sped up, making peace with mowing down the homeless, but at the last minute the raggedy man did a Macarena to the right, so that Devin and Trent barreled past him, leaving him behind as he pirouetted into a surprisingly accomplished mambo.

" 'A little bit of Monica in my life . . . ,' " the homeless man sang tunelessly, but the lawyers left him far behind as they tore down the street and reached Devin's car.

"Here!" Devin shouted, and she flung open the driver's side at the same moment that Trent sprinted for the passenger door and they both leapt inside.

Devin shoved a key into the ignition and slammed the pedal to the metal. The car lurched forward despite the snow and careered down the street until the bad guys in ski masks became tiny dots in the dark and objects in the mirror were, ironically, smaller than they appeared. Devin twisted the car through dark city streets until they had left midtown and the traffic and people in the distance.

They drove for half an hour, and in time the fancy eateries and apartment buildings gave way to fast food joints and run-down homes covered with graffiti. Devin had driven each block with one eye on the rearview mirror, and Trent had kept turning behind until he was sure they weren't being followed. They were both finally calming down, their breathing returned to normal, when they pulled up by the curb to figure what the hell was going on. "That was exciting," Devin said, meaning it.

"All except for the gun part. That was more excitement than I need."

"Ha!" Devin rested her hand on the steering wheel and caught her breath. "You did all right. Held up very well, especially for a guy who hangs with bunnies."

"You making fun of my bunny?"

"No, I'm making fun of you."

Trent smiled, despite himself. "What's up, doc?"

"What's up is I never heard of a district attorney keeping a rabbit for a pet. I mean, a Doberman, I can see. But a bunny?"

"It shows I'm sensitive."

"It shows you're stupid."

Trent fell quiet a minute. "You don't really think I had a rabbit for a pet, do you?"

"You did, until his untimely death."

"Buck was a very special rabbit."

"I'm sure. He understood you like no other mammal."

"No, not that." Trent paused. "In fact, Buck was the hippity-hoppity host for something very special, which is why I think he was killed."

"He knew too much?" Devin laughed, but Trent's face turned grave.

"His microchip did."

Devin laughed again. "You have to be kidding me."

"Not at all."

"Come on. I've heard some strange things in this case. Homicidal clowns. Missing toes. Lame lawyer jokes. But a *microchip*?"

"It's true. That's what I was going to tell you about before." Trent shifted closer and lowered his voice, though there were no passersby on the street. Not this late, not in this weather, and certainly not in this tough neighborhood. Snow fell steadily, muffling the city noises and making a hush that Trent found soothing. "You know how you can embed microchips in pets, for identification?"

"No."

"Well, you can, in the back of their necks. You have to do it, for example, if you quarantine an animal for travel abroad."

"I don't travel abroad. I drive to Hoboken. I pretend it's Paris."

Trent smiled. He liked Devin. Number one, she looked good in a hot tub. Number two, they had just come through fire together and here she was cracking jokes. But he could see she didn't believe him, and he found himself wanting her to. "Listen. There was a microchip embedded in Buck's neck that contained a set of very important documents. When they killed Buck, they took the chip."

"But why a rabbit?"

"Because no one would ever suspect it. Or so I thought."

Devin shifted over. She was intrigued. "What's on the chip?"

"Documents I was supposed to be safeguarding, that showed fraud and massive price-fixing."

"By whom?"

"By the oil industry."

Devin's mouth opened in surprise. "For real?"

"Absolutely. I'm not just an assistant D.A. I belong to an organization that . . . well, that tries to solve major problems. World-threatening problems. The oil business has been fixing prices since the days of Standard Oil. Haven't you wondered why you're paying two bucks a gallon and there's no shortage of crude? It's a damn shame and it costs the taxpayers here—and in every other state—hundreds of millions of dollars a year."

"Was Hightower Oil involved?"

"You betcha. Hightower, under King Arthur, was the ringleader of a conspiracy that included five major oil companies."

Devin gasped. "I wonder if it had anything to do with his murder."

"I don't know. It's possible."

Devin straightened in the driver's seat. It had to be true, as crazy as it sounded. And it could help her free Julia, who was innocent. "But why did you charge Julia with murder, if you know this conspiracy did it?"

"Only by charging her have we flushed them out. I never would have let it go too far. I was going to drop the charges as soon as I could."

Devin didn't know if she believed him. And she didn't like her client being used. "You played games with Julia's life."

"She played games with everyone else, and to the extent there was a price-fixing scheme, she and her family benefited from it the most."

Devin let it drop. It was no use fighting about it now. "I don't get something. Why did you have the documents?"

"We were going to bring suit. The documents were the paper trail. You know how hard it is to prove a criminal conspiracy in antitrust law. I've been building this case for the past ten years. I was just about to move on it. File the first of fifty-two lawsuits around the country, just like the state attorneys general did with the cigarette cases. Think of the damages. The suit would have cost the industry a fortune and changed the way it did business— for the better."

"Wow." Devin nodded. She had misjudged Trent. He was a smart and handsome lawyer, fighting for justice and lower gas prices. It got Devin a little hot, but she suppressed it. There was still stuff to find out. "Why put the documents on the microchip, for heaven's sake? You can't use a file cabinet like everybody else?"

"Not for this case." Trent shook his head. "We've had break-ins at the D.A.'s office over this case—even my computer files were searched. It was going to be my big case, so I kept the documents myself."

"On Buck."

"Yep. That's why I kept that bunny with me all the time. Walked him until my neighbors started looking at me funny. Now, the case is all but lost." Trent shook his head and looked over the hood of the car. Snow dusted the windshield and back window like talcum powder. The lights of a passing car shone momentarily, then disappeared as the car moved on. Trent began to feel uneasy, and the snowy hush that had earlier given him comfort now disconcerted him. "We should get going, Devin."

"But I have to figure out who's behind this. Who killed Arthur—"

"—and who were the guys in the masks, and where the

microchip is, I know." Trent glanced at the rearview mirror but it reflected only a snow-covered back window, too obscure to lend any safety. "Let's get out of here. We'll figure it out together. Tonight. Partners, okay?"

"Okay, but one last question." Devin had to know before she agreed to any partnership, whatever that meant. "What's the deal with you and Marilyn?"

"Why do you ask?" Trent noticed another set of headlights traveling slowly down the street, shining through the snowy window like a light through fog. "Forget it. We'll talk about it on the way, partner."

"Not so fast," Devin said, trying to sound casual, which wasn't her forte. "You must have known that Marilyn was Arthur's daughter."

"Of course I did. I just played her to get the information I needed."

"And did you?" Devin was too intent on the answer to notice the headlights of a car behind them, but Trent did. The car was right behind them and it wasn't moving. Why? There were plenty of other parking spaces, especially in this part of town. Trent felt his gut tense; then he heard the sound of car doors opening, swiftly and with purpose.

"Devin!" he shouted. "Hit the gas! We've been followed."

"Oh, no!" Devin twisted on the ignition.

But this time it was too late. The car doors flew open, and the next thing Devin knew, she and Trent were being dragged from the car and borne bodily into the frigid snow.

CHAPTER

11

"I'M SCARED." MARILYN Hightower's hands trembled as she groped in her Hermès purse for a cigarette. "I just know Morgan's next. Oh, God, I don't want him to die. . . ." Her groping failed for the moment and so did words.

"Morgan, why Morgan?" Robert Rutledge was puzzled.

"I'm sorry to bother you at this hour, but I just didn't know where else to go," she cried. "Mummy's run away."

Marilyn was slumped on the leather sofa in Rutledge's office wearing a rumpled gray pantsuit and white turtleneck sweater. For the first time in her life her beautiful body looked as if it had acquired some knowledge of defeat. And it had. Her whole world had come to a bloody end in one gross betrayal after another. First her daddy's gruesome murder, then her mother's indictment, then

poor Joe Kellogg. Poor loyal Joe. She shuddered to think
of the manner of his death. Then just when it looked as if
things were looking up for Julia in the trial department,
she debarked in the *Silver Girl VI* for who knew where.
It was all too much.

"Why don't you have a drink and tell me everything?"
Rutledge offered.

Marilyn shook her head. "Oh, no thanks. No drink."
She'd never drink again. She tried to collect her thoughts.
Why would anyone kill Joe? All he'd done was prepare a
silly will her father would never in a million years have
signed. Daddy was always threatening to disinherit
them, and everyone knew he never would. It had been
the family entertainment for years. That's the reason no
one took it seriously in the first place.

"You'll all be disinherited by Thanksgiving," was
what Arthur Hightower used to say with great regu-
larity. He was always *just about* to divorce Mummy and
cut Marilyn and Morgan off. The only person who actually believed him this year was the one with no Hightower Oil stock. Marilyn sniffed. It was all so cruel and
unnecessary.

"Tell me about Morgan," Rutledge urged.

"He betrayed me, Robert." And the worst of it was,
Marilyn didn't care anymore. The facts were finally
sinking in. Her daddy was dead. He couldn't revile or
protect any of them anymore. No more family games of
that sort. The new ones were much deadlier.

When Marilyn had checked at the Commodore,
she'd found out Julia had indeed debarked in the *Silver
Girl VI*. Marilyn wanted and needed her mummy now,
but once again her mummy was out of reach.

"We're all in danger," Marilyn muttered fiercely.

She wasn't quite ready to go into Morgan's marriage problems. She resumed her search for a smoke, her hands no calmer than before. All this was his fault. Marilyn didn't want to tell Robert how deeply ashamed she was of her brother's behavior, of everything stupid he'd ever done, including getting rid of poor Joe's body in the East River. Why on earth would he allow himself to be duped into doing that? He might be stupid, but he was no killer. Morgan was her only brother, but he was an idiot.

"It's a little late for that. My head is spinning. This story is so out of control. Ten devious minds have created this tangled web. Robert, it's a nightmare."

Ten. So many? "I'm so sorry, my dear," he murmured. "Please let me help you untangle."

Marilyn shook her head, furious at this soft-spoken gentleman. Who would believe it would lead to this? It was supposed to have been a lark—a way for her and Morgan, and Julia, to parlay their small ownership in Hightower Oil, that powerful holding company that was into so much more than oil these days, into some small measure of independence over their lives. Making the most of a bad situation. It was to have been a business deal, that was all. It wasn't supposed to cause all these deaths. It wasn't supposed to put her mother on death row.

RUTLEDGE CHEWED ON the inside of his cheek. He was thinking that all his life he'd been looking for a woman who could stand up to him. Someone who understood his world. Someone who could be strong and tender at the same time, who was tough but could break down with emotion when emotion was called for.

"To tell you the truth," Marilyn said, "it would have been nothing to any of us if Daddy had just divorced Julia. We weren't always so helpless, you know. Morgan had his painting. I would have gone to work. Don't laugh. Nouveau pauvre is perfectly acceptable in any circle."

"Do you see me laughing?" Rutledge said seriously.

"Well, I *would* have worked. I've always wanted to. But Daddy never wanted us to work. He liked having the family under his thumb. You didn't know him like we did."

"Well, I knew him for a stubborn man," Rutledge murmured. "I'm sorry it's turned out this way, really I am." And he was sorry he'd doubted her, too. His informers had suspected that Marilyn was the murderer. That is, until Joe's severed hand turned up. Then he'd known a wider conspiracy was involved. The O. He glanced at his watch. He'd received a call from his "facilitators." As usual they'd made a mess of it. Paying for the cleanup would no doubt be expensive. Those guys just couldn't do anything the normal way. A simple assignment for them had to be complicated by ski masks and pistols shot into the air. They so loved crashing through windows, chasing people down fire escapes and pulling them out of their cars. Mafioso wannabes. So childish. All he wanted was to talk to them. Still, the job was done, and Trent and that defense lawyer, Devin, would be here soon. He was not sorry Marilyn would be with him when they arrived.

"Mummy wasn't always so completely wasted," Marilyn was saying. "She was a good mummy when we were little. Really. She used to care about all sorts of things. The ecology. Global warming. Do you mind?" She finally located the cigarettes at the bottom of her purse and held up the pack.

"No, no, of course not," Rutledge murmured. With a manicured finger, he pushed across the table a large crystal ashtray that had never been sullied by an ash. Until this second he'd loathed smokers.

"Mummy used to take care of us herself before she got so bitter. Most women do better with this kind of thing these days. Men can be such rats."

"I'm so sorry," Rutledge murmured again, thinking he wasn't a rat.

"I hated her for drinking." Marilyn had trouble with her lighter, so Rutledge took it out of her hand and leaned forward in his club chair to light the Benson & Hedges that wobbled between her fingers. Their knees touched, and the meltdown continued.

"I feel terrible that Morgan and I sided with you in the takeover." Marilyn inhaled deeply, saw him wince, and immediately put out the cigarette.

And she was *thoughtful*. "Marilyn, you have nothing to reproach yourself for." Robert found himself looking at her with awe. Marilyn Hightower in a state of terror, sorry about her mother and worried about her brother, was as irresistible to him as she had been unappealing to him before. Marilyn Hightower rumpled and weeping, coming to him for consolation and advice. The girl whom he'd pegged as a block of ice, who'd slept her way through the upper and lower ends of society just for the sheer fun of it, was certainly softened now. As a cold and calculating tart, she'd been nothing to him but an object of contempt. But now he could see he'd underestimated her. He hadn't known a thing about the real woman.

"Oh, I do reproach myself. We did it for business, just the way Daddy did. Daddy hurt people all the time with his little business tricks. Price-fixing oil. Cornering the market in tin or whatever it was. Well, that's pretty bad, isn't it, when you think about it?"

"It all depends on the context," Rutledge murmured.

"Oh?" Marilyn glanced at the crushed cigarette with regret.

He shrugged again. "AT&T, Bell Atlantic, Microsoft, IBM in the past, Sotheby's. The railroads. The banks, the steel fortunes. Hotel chains. Airlines. Monopoly is America's favorite game both in the drawing room and in real life. Shutting Hightower down only opens the door for others to organize. Hightower and the rest of the oil companies are nothing compared to the Arab interests. They have our whole country in a twist. Perhaps the State Department will have something to say about this. They're not supposed to murder, you know." He lifted his shoulder. Business was hell.

Marilyn's tears came again. "I never thought Morgan would kill anyone. I never thought Mummy would be accused." She swiped at her lovely eyes with the handkerchief. Rutledge wondered if he could take her hand. Maybe in a minute.

"You should have come to me with all this sooner," he said.

"I suspected you were with the bad guys, Robert. You were having me followed, after all." She blew her nose and gave him the knowing look of the old Marilyn.

He coughed again. "It doesn't do to underestimate the players," he told her gently.

"So it *was* you." Her clear-eyed glance cut through him. "I've been sold down the river," she cried.

"Marilyn, who killed your father?"

"I'm sure you thought I did. I certainly thought *you* did." Marilyn put her hand to her brow. "My pearls were the ones found in Daddy's hand. They weren't Julia's at all." She swallowed hard. "And Trent persuaded me to let them indict Mummy to flush out the real killer."

Rutledge nodded. "Yes, so you said."

"I'm scared." Marilyn trembled. "I don't know why I agreed to put Mummy in such jeopardy."

"Who, Marilyn? Tell me."

"Sissy." Marilyn whispered finally, glancing around fearfully as if the room might be bugged.

"Sissy? Morgan's wife?"

"She's really weird, Robert. She carries a gun." Marilyn's eyes circuited the room again. "And that 'dumb tart' thing is just an act."

Rutledge nodded again. The "dumb tart" thing was an act with many women, Marilyn included. He was learning the hard way. But he did know of Sissy's sex shop.

"Now, with Daddy's death and your takeover, Sissy stands to inherit hundreds of millions with Morgan. The problem is, he plans to divorce her."

"Does he know she's the killer?"

Marilyn shook her head. "I don't know what he knows. But I heard her screaming at him, having a *complete* freak-out."

"Why?"

"Morgan was having an affair with Cordelia. They'd been together for years. I wouldn't be surprised if he was secretly *married* to Cordelia. He'd only had that ridiculous ceremony with Sissy to infuriate Daddy. Morgan has no idea who Sissy is."

Rutledge's body tensed. "Are you talking about my Cordelia?"

"*Your* Cordelia?" Marilyn snorted. "More like anybody's Cordelia. The first time I saw Cordelia she was doing it with Daddy. On the *Silver Girl V*, of course. The woman likes the water."

"The Cordelia who works for me?" Rutledge was astounded. Here was something he didn't know.

"The very same. Cordelia is the mother of Morgan's baby."

"Cordelia has a *baby*?" Rutledge scratched his head in wonder. And he'd thought he screened his employees so well. "How do you know this?" he asked.

"I like the water, too, Robert. People at the Commodore are my friends. I know Mummy took off from there. So did Morgan. I'll probably never see poor Mummy again. Maybe she intends to sink the yacht." More tears for Julia.

"Why don't you tell the police all this, Marilyn?"

"Sissy *is* the police. She killed my daddy. If we don't stop her she'll certainly kill Morgan for cheating her out of the big money. The man who killed Joe is with the police, too. And somebody persuaded Morgan to dump his body in the river, probably Cordelia. Some detective with a hook is investigating. Have you noticed how weak the investigation is? The whole police involvement is missing a limb. Trent Ballard is with the D.A.'s office. And you've probably known this all along." Finally Marilyn accused him straight out.

It was very late now, and Rutledge was breathing

hard. He was glad that Marilyn had finally come to him. He marveled at her brains. This girl had wasted her talents on flirtation with nobodies. She should be in his organization. She should be a CEO. She should be his wife if she would have him. Her skills in detection were better than his thousand-dollar-a-day detectives. He was in wonderment at her. He wanted to embrace Marilyn and propose to her on the spot, but the phone rang before he had a chance.

He picked up on the first ring. "Rutledge." Then he listened for a moment and his face paled.

"Who is this? Oh, my God." When he hung up he said gently, "Morgan's dead. I'm so sorry."

At last he had the honor of Marilyn completely collapsing in his arms.

IN THE HOSPITAL, Patrick's teeth were chattering again. He may have sounded like the parody of a wooden puppet manifesting fear, but he was no longer fearful. He was a man now. He had a woman to comfort and a job to do, and he wanted to get on with it. And he was stuck in a treatment room with his clothes off. Chatter, chatter, he couldn't get the words to freedom out of his mouth.

A few short days ago he'd had ten toes and a nothing occupation that paid him close to zip. He'd longed to be a reporter. He'd had no dates since he couldn't remember when. Thirty-one years old, and the extent of Patrick Roswell's kicks in life had been hamburgers and drinks at Sweeney's. He admitted it. He'd been a wimp and a wuss and only dared to kiss the girl of his dreams in the Taurus because their cover was about to be blown. Then, right after the kiss, she'd sent him off into the night, like the true hero he was, to face certain death with dignity. Love was so fleeting.

He'd lived, if not exactly triumphed. He still had no job and only nine toes, but he was lucky he wasn't missing any other body parts, considering the fact that Joe Kellogg had lost both his hand and his head, and the rest of him was nothing but fish food in the East River. If there were any fish in the East River. Maybe the eels were eating his bits. Somewhere he'd read that eels were the only thing that could survive in such pollution. He'd have to look it up someday. What a story this was going to make!

Patrick had thought he'd never get the feeling of Devin's kiss, or the image of Joe Kellogg's head escaping from the ice chest, out of his head. But then he'd suffered a forced visit into the murky deep himself. The river water was so frigid at this time of the year it had almost stopped his heart. Patrick knew the taste of torture and terror. He'd had a near-death experience and the sweet agony of a return to life through the magnificent power of passionate physical love. Julia's and his. Perfect in its nuttiness and brevity. When he persuaded her to return to court and reveal everything she didn't even know she knew, he'd felt he was saving her very soul. Such experiences didn't happen every day.

He couldn't help composing the story for Devin and the world. He'd reveal it in all its deadly facets. To die and live again. To see a woman of Julia's caliber lose her son. Story upon story he had to tell.

Julia had given Patrick the clothes of her dead husband, Arthur. Arthur had been a large and beefy man. His togs, all cashmere, linen, and silk, hadn't fit Patrick. But Patrick had been warmed by them, and now they were gone. He was stuck in a treatment room, shivering and shaking while two doctors who looked twelve years old stood around him shaking their heads over his various injuries, including the missing toe, which seemed to baffle them.

"How'd you lose that toe?" asked the taller of the two.

"Ba Ba Ba," chatter, chatter, chatter. Patrick had to get out of there and find Devin.

He was bundled up in electric blankets. It was not as pleasant as being in Julia's berth, but pretty toasty nevertheless. An IV was stuck in a vein in his hand. His eyelids fluttered. Still, with the doctors hanging over him like that, demanding information, it was a lot like being with that clown the toe cutter. It occurred to him that maybe they weren't really doctors. Maybe they were more clowns in doctor suits. He was hallucinating. Where was Julia? Where was Devin? "Don't touch me," he screamed, but only in his head.

"Gotta go," he managed to get out. "Gimme my clothes." He had to tell Devin about Morgan and Cordelia. About Morgan's throwing Joe's remains in the river. And also how he almost died before finding himself and writing the book that would win him a Pulizer prize. And of course before telling her she was the one he loved. Before telling about . . . Julia's magnificent sacrifice in saving him! Patrick's eyes popped open. He'd never tell Devin or anybody else about those brief, perfect moments with Julia! Never tell, never . . . his eyes drooped again. He was lost in author's dreamland, busy writing the story that would make his career.

*   *   *

JULIA HIGHTOWER SAT in a turquoise molded plastic chair in the ER's waiting room at Long Island General Hospital bowed with grief. The sharp mind that had clung to anesthesia as the therapy of choice for too many years was awakening. Patrick Roswell (the momentary aberration who had sobered her up as nothing else ever had) was off somewhere being treated for insanity as well as hypothermia. He thought he was Truman Capote. So sad.

Lined up across the back wall of the room, flanking the sliding doors and all other exits, a whole regiment of police were blocking her escape. They should be treated for madness as well. They were acting as if she were Bonnie and Clyde rolled into one, had managed to kill her own son as well as her husband and any second would try to make a getaway so she could kill some more. She shivered at the very thought.

Her phone call to Devin had yielded an answering machine message and no reply as yet. She'd been told that her daughter had been located and was on her way. There was nothing left to do but wait. Julia was hungry but didn't recognize the feeling as the need for food. Her head ached. She would give her whole fortune for a chance to replay the family's last fatal reunion. She glanced up, searching for Marilyn, her last living relative, but saw only detectives. They were odd-looking men. One had a hook instead of an arm. He'd already tried to question her about the death of her son, but she wasn't going to be an active participant in her own destruction any longer. Julia was sober and angry enough now to keep her mouth zipped shut. She needed help this time. She wasn't blabbing to the enemy. Waves of grief and rage lashed at her.

Harcourt was DOA. He didn't have a thing to tell them. He'd been downstairs in the hall. He must have opened the door to the killer. Or else the killer had been in the house already and had felled him on the way out. Who had a motive to kill Morgan? Who would gain from his death? Only one person. It wasn't a hard one.

Julia was furious at the bad girls of the world. Look how they'd ruined her life! The women who married for money, like Sissy; the women who slept with other people's husbands. She wasn't paying blackmail to one of her own jury. She wasn't talking to flatfoots who were so dim they refused to see that she was incapable of killing a germ, much less a human being. She was talking to Devin, her counsel.

In that blue plastic chair, surrounded by cops, Julia had a sudden flash. She'd tell Devin the truth about her own legacy. She'd insist that Devin sort out the legal questions of blackmail, her false arrest. Everything. She'd have Marilyn and Devin work out the will and business issues together. It was time for the good girls to take their place in the world, to stand up for themselves and make themselves useful. To prevail.

As Julia waited for her girls to arrive, she had other thoughts, too. Being rich wasn't as easy as people thought. Everyone they knew bowed and scraped, of course, but let's face it—no one really liked the rich. She never had liked them much herself. She may have been excited and corrupted by wealth. She'd married the wrong man and allowed herself to be degraded by it, just as Arthur had lost touch with himself in his lust for money and power. Both of them had been disappointed when wealth didn't bring the happiness they'd dreamed of. But neither had been able to do a thing about it. There wasn't a course in every school on how to be a well-adjusted rich person. Money had paralyzed them, and now all the men were gone.

Julia could see activity outside the ER entrance. There was movement with those cops. She imagined herself as the football at a college homecoming. The cops were coming to take her away, to punish her for her selfishness, her sins of omission. Her eyes were puffy. Her heart was heavy. She needed a drink but would never have one again. She wanted to tell someone she was a good girl. She was one of the good ones. The tension built up inside her until she felt she would explode. Then the doors slid open and together Marilyn, Devin, and Robert Rutledge rushed into the waiting room. Marilyn saw her first and oblivious to the uniformed cops, the detective with the hook, the nurses and doctors, the gurneys and late-night emergencies, she cried out, "Mummy, hang in there. I love you."

Julia, pretty shocky to begin with, fell off her chair.

CHAPTER

12

THE FOOD IN the hospital commissary was bad, and the coffee was worse, but after all this group of people had been through, they barely noticed. All of them—Devin and Patrick, Julia and Marilyn, Rutledge and Harrison—huddled around a Formica-topped table . sharing secrets, slowly unraveling the tangled web that had ensnared them all.

Harrison snapped his cell phone closed, punctuating their conversation with a decided click. "Got her!"

"Sissy?" Marilyn asked.

"Right. State patrolman nabbed her just before she crossed the New Jersey border."

"Send the poor man backup," Rutledge muttered. "She's dangerous."

"You don't have to tell me. I've known her a long time." Harrison grinned. "I understand she practically crippled the first guy who found her. Took three of them to get the cuffs on her. But they managed."

"So I was right," Marilyn said. "Sissy's a cop."

Harrison craned his neck. "She's . . . something like a cop. Or was, anyway."

"She's in the O, isn't she?" Rutledge said. "And unless I miss my guess, you are, too. Admit it."

Harrison arched an eyebrow, apparently surprised that Rutledge knew the O existed. "I'm afraid I can neither confirm nor deny that."

"Tell us more about Sissy," Julia implored. "Are you saying she was . . . undercover? That she only married my son to get information?"

"She was never supposed to marry him," Harrison explained. "I don't know how that happened. At first, I thought maybe she really liked him. Now it seems clear she saw an opportunity to make a big score—bigger than she had dreamed possible."

"By killing my husband," Julia said.

Harrison nodded solemnly. "And arranging it so that you would be convicted. Leaving Marilyn and her brother to inherit."

Marilyn covered her face with her hand. "I knew that Morgan was scheming to gain control of the corporation. But I never imagined that his wife had killed Daddy." She paused, gathering her strength. "Morgan and I talked about some sort of takeover scheme to convert our interest in Hightower Oil into cash. I knew he had his mistress, Cordelia, lure Daddy to the Sweeney Hotel. She plied Daddy with liquor, then arranged to have a lookalike of Mr. Rutledge persuade him to sign some papers. He told Daddy the papers were just pro forma corporate documents, but actually they transferred control of Hightower Oil to Morgan. Daddy was too smart for them, though—even liquored up."

"So Sissy knocked him over the head?"

"I guess so. She had access to the freezer key, of course. And it was a cinch for her to snag all the matching pearl necklaces and to smear blood on one of Mummy's dresses."

"And I'll bet she put the bomb in my car, too. She didn't want Julia getting exonerated. She wanted her locked away for as long as possible."

Marilyn nodded. "I knew Morgan wanted the money—but I didn't realize what he was willing to do to get it. I'm so sorry, Mummy."

"Don't torture yourself, dear," Julia said. "You didn't know."

"But that isn't the worst of it," Marilyn continued. "When the Sweeney Hotel scam didn't play, Morgan and I allowed Mummy to be charged, even though we knew she wasn't guilty, so that we would gain control of the corporation, if only temporarily."

"How could you know it would be temporary?"

"I had . . . inside information. I knew Mummy had been at the spa at the time of death. And I had . . . talked to Trent Ballard, the assistant D.A. handling the case. He assured me the charges were brought only to flush out the true killer. So I thought as long as he's using this charge for his own benefit, why shouldn't we?" She looked up, her eyes wide and watery. "I'm so sorry, Mummy."

Julia reached out and squeezed her daughter's hand. "We've all made mistakes, dear. Let's just put them behind us."

"So what happened to Kellogg?" Devin asked. "Why

did that psycho kill him? How did Morgan end up with the body?"

"The psycho?" Julia asked. "Who's this?"

"The clown," Devin explained. "Fran, the Foot Locker employee." She turned toward Harrison. "He works for your mysterious little organization, doesn't he?"

Harrison nodded slowly. "Or did, anyway, until he got on the wrong side of Sissy." He glanced down at his hook. "Not that the world is going to miss him much. He didn't kill Kellogg, though. He may have tortured and maimed him—to send Mr. Rutledge here a message—but he didn't kill him."

"Then who did?"

"Morgan," Patrick said firmly. "With Sissy's help, probably. I saw him dispose of the body."

"But why?"

"I think I can answer that," Rutledge said. "Joe had been in on Morgan's scheme from the first, since Cordelia lured him to the Sweeney to help out with the attempted scam on Arthur. And he stayed a part of it. Who knows what Morgan offered him—a big chunk of the company, probably. But the guilt was eating him up. He was threatening to talk. He called me and said he had something important to tell me. But he never made it to my office. After the clown cut off his hand, Sissy and Morgan must've finished him off. That's why he couldn't tell you where Kellogg's body was, Patrick. He didn't know. He hadn't killed him."

"Why did he torture me? Why did he cut off my toe?"

"He saw you talking with Joe in a bar. He assumed you were involved in the illegal scheme that Joe was perpetrating with Arthur Hightower"—he glanced at Rutledge—"among others. When he found out otherwise, he cut you loose—although not until after conning you into trying to frame me."

"Why would he do that?"

Harrison shrugged. "Old business. Goes way back. It doesn't matter. One reason or the other, Joe Kellogg is still dead."

"Poor Joe," Julia murmured. "He didn't deserve that."

"Same fate for Morgan, I'm guessing," Harrison said. "Maybe he was threatening to talk. Maybe Sissy just thought he was too dangerous to live. Whatever the reason—she knocked him off. And fled."

"And Harcourt?"

"I can't say for sure. But judging from the evidence at the crime scene, I suspect Harcourt was just in the wrong place at the wrong time. He saw too much—so Sissy had to kill him."

"I still don't understand what this secret organization was doing. Sissy, the clown, you." Patrick leaned toward Harrison. "Why are you people involved?"

"I'm afraid I can't answer that," Harrison replied.

"Come on. At least give me a clue. I'm good with clues."

Harrison took a deep breath, then released it. "Let's just say that Arthur Hightower—with the assistance of the late Joe Kellogg and Mr. Rutledge here—was engaged in some extremely illegal activities. Activities that could not be permitted to proceed any further. Activities that threatened the global economy—the safety of the world itself."

"Oh, don't be so melodramatic," Rutledge said.

"I'm not. Do you have any idea what you've been playing with? You may think you're just a couple of good ol' boys trying to make a buck with a little old-fashioned price-fixing, but what you're doing could destabilize nations. Not only large ones, but Third World nations. Middle Eastern nations. Nations that are dangerous. Nations with more weapons than they know what to do with. Your activities could put millions of lives at risk."

Rutledge drew himself up. "You have no proof that I was involved in any of this."

"You mean because you had your thugs steal the microchip?" Harrison smiled thinly. "Yes, I know about that. Did you honestly think we wouldn't make copies? Trent is a good operative, in an eccentric sort of way, but no one is infallible."

"If you had any proof, we wouldn't be having this conversation. You have nothing."

"You're wrong. Maybe we don't have enough to go to court, but we have more than enough to know that you're guilty as sin. And to try to stop it. You're a dangerous man, Mr. Rutledge." He leaned in closer. "And mark my words, you will be stopped."

"Don't you dare threaten me, you hook-handed punk. I'll eat you for breakfast." He rose quickly to his feet. "If you try to smear me or accuse me or . . . or . . . inconvenience me in any way, I'll make you wish you'd never been born. I've got friends, see? Lots of friends, in high places. I'm untouchable. So you might as well find someone else to intimidate. Because you don't scare me." He drew his greatcoat tighter around himself. "Marilyn, I'll call you tomorrow."

Marilyn looked away. "Robert . . . please don't."

For a moment, he seemed genuinely saddened. "Very well. As you wish." He pushed away from the table and made his way out of the commissary.

"Devin," Julia announced, "as soon as the charges against me are dropped and the jury is dismissed, I want you to take something to a man named Jack Powell for me."

"Okay. What is it?"

"A check."

Devin's eyes widened. "You're not going to pay blackmail money to that juror, are you?"

"Blackmail, no. After the charges are dropped, he will have no claim on me. This money is for his half brother—Arthur's son. I've known of his existence for some time, but I was too cowardly to do anything about it. No longer. From now on, the Hightowers start taking responsibility for their actions."

"It's hard to believe," Patrick murmured, "but I think I finally understand what went on here."

"There's one thing I don't understand," Julia said.

"What's that, Mummy?"

Her eyes turned downward. "How I could have raised such an evil son."

Marilyn wanted to comfort her, but she knew there was nothing to say. Instead, she clung tightly to her mother's hand, squeezing it, letting her love flow through her to her parent. It wasn't much. But at the moment, it was all she had to give.

As ROBERT RUTLEDGE strode confidently into the chilly night, he was being watched by a pair of dark eyes that managed to stay close without ever being noticed. Most of the time, he favored more flamboyant disguises, but for a stalking job, the basic ninja black was best. He was

very good at being invisible, when he wanted to be. And
at the moment, he wanted to be.

So you think you're invincible, do you? the man
known as Stefan thought as he watched Rutledge make
his way to his car. Well, so did Sissy, and she's going
down for the count. So did Arthur Hightower and Joe
Kellogg, come to think of it. And they're both history.
And so are you.

He would wait until the right moment. The right moment to tell the O he was still around (as if a lightweight
like Sissy could seriously damage him) and the right moment to finish his job. Because he always finished his
jobs. It was a matter of pride for him. He didn't care that
much about financial markets, or global price-fixing, or
the security of the Middle East. But he cared about his
job record. Never in his distinguished career had he left a
job unfinished.

And Robert Rutledge would be no exception.

DESPITE THE BRACING cold, Devin had asked Patrick to
walk her home, and he had eagerly accepted. He'd been
through a lot in the past forty-eight hours—torture, mu-
tilation, freezing-cold water, even a wild fling with an el-
derly society matron. But now that the shouting was
over, now that they were alone, one thought seemed
paramount—he really liked Devin McGee. But what
chance did he have with a smart, attractive professional
like her? How could she ever be interested in a dull advertising salesman who dabbled in crosswords?

"Thank you for walking me home," Devin said. Her
breath formed little clouds in front of her mouth. "It's
not far."

"I don't mind," he said quietly.

"I know it's an imposition. But I—I just didn't want to be alone right now."

"Sure. I understand."

"Do you?" Her shoulder brushed against his. Patrick felt a chill run up his spine, and it wasn't due to the temperature. "I mean, you've got this great glamorous job at the paper, selling ads and investigating stories. You're surrounded by people all the time. I'm on my own. Have been for years. Don't even have a receptionist. Some mornings I wake up and I ask, Devin Gail McGee, what have you done to yourself?"

Patrick couldn't believe his ears. This gorgeous lawyer thought his job was glamorous? "You have clients. Other lawyers . . ."

"Oh, sure. People who want something from me. People who are fighting me. It isn't the same. Not like the fast-paced life in the newsroom."

"You know . . . I told you I don't normally do news stories—"

"You will. After you break this story, you'll be big time."

Patrick swallowed. Could she be right? "Mostly I just sell ad copy. And do the crossword."

She smiled. "I like to work crosswords, too."

Patrick winced. Obviously, she misunderstood what he meant by "doing" the crossword.

"In fact," Devin continued, "I actually construct crosswords."

Patrick stopped in his tracks. "You construct crosswords?"

"Oh, yeah. Every now and again. Just a spare-time thing, when I don't have any pressing cases. I've got an unfinished crossword grid I've been carrying around in my briefcase for days."

"But—are your puzzles published?"

"Oh, yeah. I've been pretty successful. I've been in the *New York Times*. *Games* magazine."

"You have?" Patrick literally gaped. "But—I haven't seen your name on a byline."

"Oh, you wouldn't. I use a pseudonym. I do crosswords under the name Isolde."

Patrick grabbed Devin by the shoulders. "You're Isolde?"

"Yes. Why?"

He shook her, so excited he could barely stand still. "You're Isolde?"

"I think I said that already."

"*I'm Tristan!*"

It took a moment for his words to register—then her lips turned upward in a huge grin. "You're kidding me."

"No! I'm Tristan! I named myself after you! You're my hero!"

Devin shuffled her feet. "Oh, go on."

"Seriously! I think you're the best crossword constructor working today."

"Really?" She tilted her head to one side. "Well, you're no slouch yourself. I loved that themed puzzle you did with the punny names of breakfast cereals. 'Trix of the Trade,' and such."

"Well, that was nothing compared to that diagramless you did where the grid was in the shape of the Empire State Building."

"Did you like that?"

"I thought it was awesome."

"I guess we have more in common than I realized."

She smiled, then pressed her hand against his. "Patrick, I don't want to seem presumptuous, but do you suppose two crossword constructors could ever find happiness together?"

"I know they could," he replied quietly.

"How can you know?"

"Your name. It's an anagram."

"It is?"

"Sure. 'Devin Gail' anagrams to 'Divine Gal.' Which you certainly are."

Devin grinned. "When did you work that out?"

"The second I met you."

She laughed. "We crossword people are a strange bunch."

"I think it's kismet."

She took his gloved hand and resumed walking. "You know, Patrick, I'm not sleepy. And I'm not in the mood to be alone. Would you like to come up to my apartment?"

Patrick gulped. "Sure!"

"Good. I'd like that."

As they strolled the last block to Devin's apartment, a light snow began to fall. The garbage men came out and started rattling down the streets in their noisy trucks. A siren sounded two streets over.

And Tristan and Isolde never noticed any of it.

THANKSGIVING DAY. A time when families all across the country spend quality time together delighting in one another's company. This Thanksgiving, at the Hightower mansion, an extended family gathered harmoniously.

Not only were Julia and Marilyn Hightower present, but also newlyweds Devin and Patrick Roswell.

"Thank you so much for joining us," Julia Hightower said as she sat down at the head of the table. "The room would've seemed so empty without you. And we need to catch up."

"It's our pleasure," Devin replied. She marveled at how healthy Julia looked. Word was she hadn't had a drink since she learned Morgan was dead. And Marilyn looked fabulous as well. "What else would we be doing? Fast food?"

"I think our spread will be better than that," Marilyn said.

"Actually, Patrick is a rather good cook."

"Indeed?"

Patrick blushed. "Well, all I know how to make are cheeseburgers."

"Yes," Devin said, "but they're damn fine cheeseburgers."

"I love cheeseburgers," Marilyn said. "Invite me over sometime."

"You have a standing invite," Devin replied. "You and Trent both."

Now it was Marilyn's turn to blush. "You heard about that."

"I did. And I think he's a very lucky man." Just don't let him near a hot tub, she added silently.

"I don't want to make too much of it," Marilyn said, although she clearly did. "But it is nice." She smiled at Patrick. "How's life for the *Gazette*'s cub reporter?"

"Great. After the series I wrote on the murders, Whitechapel will let me cover anything I want. More than I want, really. Devin's practice boomed after all the publicity Julia's case received. For a while there, I barely heard from her, except when she needed a three-letter word with no vowels."

Marilyn rolled her eyes. "You crossword people are just too weird."

Patrick grinned. "Hey, I don't want to be rude, but can I ask a question?"

"Of course."

"Why is there a fifth place set at the table?"

All eyes turned toward the empty chair with the fine china and goblet set before it.

Julia explained. "I invited Georges, our gardener."

Marilyn looked horrified. "Mummy! You didn't!"

"I'm afraid I did. I know it might be a bit awkward for you, dear—and for me as well—but he is our only remaining staff person, and I just couldn't see letting him eat downstairs by himself. So I sent him an invitation."

"Where is he? I never knew him to turn down a good meal."

"I don't know." Julia checked her watch. "He is somewhat overdue."

Marilyn gazed out the window. "Come to think of it, where has he been lately? I haven't seen him around. And the yard looks terrible. And—"

She stopped short. Julia and Marilyn exchanged a look.

"You don't suppose."

"Don't be ridiculous."

Devin intervened. "What are you two talking about?"

Slowly, Julia rose to her feet and walked into the kitchen. She returned an instant later, her arms akimbo.

"All right," she said firmly, "who's got the freezer key this time?"

AFTERWORD

THIS BOOK EXISTS for two reasons—because Phillip Margolin is such a nice guy, and because Brita Cantrell makes the world's best margarita. Brita is also nice, and Phillip may make a swell margarita for all I know, but that isn't really relevant.

A few years ago, I edited a collection of legal-themed short stories that was published under the title *Legal Briefs*. Putting that book together was tough and time-consuming, but it was a labor of love. Having the opportunity to work with so many of the most talented writers of our time could only be a delight for a long-term bookworm like me. I was proud of the book that resulted, but I was especially pleased after its publication, when the aforementioned Mr. Margolin sent me a note that read: *That was fun. We should do it again sometime.*

Phillip had good reason to enjoy the anthology; his

contribution was chosen for the *Best American Mystery Stories of 1999*. Still, the idea resonated with me. Do it again? An interesting idea, but I didn't want to repeat myself with another short story collection. Was there some other kind of joint project?

About that time, my wife and I were invited to dinner by our good friends Daman and Brita Cantrell, an invitation irresistible because, among other reasons, Brita makes the previously described potent potable. At the time, Brita was the state director of The Nature Conservancy, and during dinner she mentioned some of the wonderful projects they wanted to tackle, untouched lands they wanted to preserve—but couldn't, because they didn't have the funds.

Those who have read my novel *Dark Justice* will know that environmental causes are close to my heart. Surely, I thought, there must be some way to raise those funds. . . .

And all at once, in a wonderful moment of serendipity, the two ideas merged into one. And this book is the result.

Was it hard to get all these major authors to donate their time and talent to a project on which they would make nary a penny? No. In my experience, writers are among the most generous groups in our populace. As a result, I was in the happy position of being able to pick exactly who I wanted to join me, ten of the most talented writers working today.

When I first approached the authors, I thought we might all get together on a conference call and hash out the story. As it turned out, no one wanted to do that. Just send me the chapters that came before, they all said. It'll be more fun if I get it cold.

They were right. In the end, there were no rules, restrictions, guidelines, or caveats. Each author was limited only by his or her imagination—and the need to make the next chapter sensible in light of what had gone before. Basically, they could do anything they wanted—and did. I wrote the first chapter, trying to create some characters and situations with untapped possibilities, then shipped it to the next author in line—who wrote chapter 2, and sent it to the next author. And so forth. That's how *Natural Suspect* came to be.

Was I surprised by the final product? You betcha. I won't name names, but what some of these authors did to my characters was strange and savage, if not altogether perverse. Compare where the book is at the end of chapter 1 to where it is at the end of, say, chapter 7, and you'll see what I mean. Killer clowns? Giant rabbits? But the strangest thing is—every expansion and innovation made the book better. And think about those chapter-end cliff-hangers. Some of these authors, obviously, were taking delight in giving the next writer on the list a challenging situation. Which made the book better still.

I was somewhat prejudiced, of course, but when it was all finished, I thought it read remarkably well—with consistent characters and a well-developed plot. As a test, before I sent the manuscript to my publisher, I asked three of my friends to read it, without explaining the book's provenance. All three liked it, but more to the point—not one of them suspected it had been written by multiple authors.

*   *   *

SOME READERS MAY wish to know more about The Nature Conservancy and their important role in preserving our natural heritage, or may wish to make tax-deductible contributions. You can do both at: The Nature Conservancy, 2727 East 21st Street, Suite 102, Tulsa, Oklahoma 74114. Or call 1(918)585-1117. Or you can visit their Web site: http://www.tnc.org/. Tell them *Natural Suspect* sent you.

Thanks for being a part of this fun project. I hope you enjoyed the book. If you'd like to share your thoughts about it, e-mail me at: wb@williambernhardt.com. Or you can visit my Web site: www. williambernhardt.com, where you will find links to the Web pages of many of the other authors in this book.

—William Bernhardt

THE MYSTERY WITHIN THE MYSTERY ...

Can you guess which author
wrote which chapter of *Natural Suspect*?
For the opportunity to play detective
(and win valuable prizes), log on to

www.naturalsuspect.com

for details.